THE
HAREM
GAMES

JORGE CARRERAS JR.

outskirtspress
DENVER, COLORADO

The Harem Games
All Rights Reserved.
Copyright © 2013 Jorge Carreras Jr.
v2.0

Cover Photo © 2013 Jorge Carreras Jr. All rights reserved - used with permission.

Outskirts Press, Inc.
http://www.outskirtspress.com

Paperback ISBN: 978-1-4787-1107-0
Hardback ISBN: 978-1-4327-9453-8

Outskirts Press and the "OP" logo are trademarks belonging to Outskirts Press, Inc.

PRINTED IN THE UNITED STATES OF AMERICA

Author's Note

I have drawn the inspiration from this work from many and various sources.

If you find something that "rings true" with your favorite genre, book, movie, or other work, please take this in the spirit in which it is intended.

Special Thanks

To all my friends and family who have supported me through my
many years.

Prologue

Harem: A single person being pursued romantically by numerous members of the opposite sex simultaneously. Usually one male pursued by numerous females.

A female pursued by numerous males also existed, but generally speaking, didn't end well among humans. A single female with multiple mates doesn't lead to more offspring while a single male with multiple females does. That's the hard fact about the biology.

With the extreme scarcity of males amongst the population, it currently isn't a viable construct either.

Games: 1.) An activity pursued strictly for the sake of pleasure. Example: a game of solitaire.

2.) A contest, competition, or ritual designed to settle conflict in an enclosed environment under certain rules and conditions. Example: the Olympic Games.

Unfortunately, there are far too many people who, using the first definition, think that a "game" is always something unimportant. This is far from the case. Just because something is a "game," doesn't mean it can't be deadly serious; in fact, "war games" are military training exercises, and thinking of them as unimportant could get people killed.

Further, falling under the second definition, there are ritualistic "games" where contestants have to be the last "survivor" in order to win, whether it's surviving against a deadly environment or against each other.

The "Harem Games" falls under both of those conditions. Participants have to fight each other and the environment in a deadly struggle for survival with the last remaining survivor and his harem being declared the winner.

How did things get this way? Well, I, Martufe O'oharra, an actual survivor of M-Day, as well as "patient zero," am the only one who can tell that story. Today's date is July 4, 200 A.M. (After Man).

A little over two hundred years ago, an unknown agent began attacking the human population of Earth. The true nature of the pathogen is unknown. The result of the pandemic, however, is quite well known. Although it made me quite immortal and sterile (there's been no lack of people trying to prove this statement false), for the rest of the population, it's been horrifying.

First, all men who were past puberty just died overnight, apparently at random. No symptoms of any kind were reported.

"How was I chosen as 'patient zero' then?"

I DID show symptoms and, rather severe ones, numerous coronary failures, seizures, simultaneous multiple organ failures, and so on. All of these corrected themselves, which baffled every single doctor and nurse working on my case.

Second result.

Young males lived normally until reaching puberty, then weakened and eventually died.

Third result.

The viability of male offspring in the womb plummeted. Male children would be born literally heartless, and the boy's body would immediately reject any artificial heart placed within it. There is the rare one- in- a- million exception where a viable male birth would occur, or none of you would be here. Every attempt at trying to solve the problem met with dismal failure despite the very best and brightest working at it, continuously, tirelessly, day and night.

Fourth result.

The viability of pregnancy among women increased exponentially. Originally, women were only fertile once a month, and conception could be prevented using contraception. This is no longer the case.

Women are now fertile once a week, contraception in all forms is no longer effective, contact with sperm in any way could result in pregnancy, and gestation has shrunk from nine months to nine weeks because the fetus grows very quickly.

Very quickly, women took control of political power in every nation for the simple reason that there were no men who could run things. In many countries, previously, women were treated very badly.

China and India, as they were once known, were prime examples. China's "one child" population control policy led to the near genocide of female children as, obviously, it's the male children who carried on the family name. India had a near genocide among women for a different reason. Originally, husbands would be given a dowry by the girl's family, presumably to help provide for her. Eventually, though, society began to see giving birth to girls as "shameful."

So the meaning of the dowry became twisted. For poor families who produced daughters and could not afford a dowry, it came to mean

"We are so disgraced by our daughter that we're PAYING you to get rid of her." Some men were even on record setting their wives on fire, burning them alive.

Naturally, the women from these countries wanted revenge, and after finding out that their daughters' fertility increased exponentially, they began their "sacred crusade."

Oh, this change did not come quietly. There was fierce opposition. Most notably, and to its eternal credit, the former United States, was the very loudest in opposing this "plan."

Its reasoning was two-fold.

First, putting aside a very loud but very small minority of man-hating feminists, the women there were quite happy with their men and how they were treated. Women were treated as equals as much as humanly possible. Obviously men couldn't give birth, for example. So it was a civil rights issue.

Second, considering the rarity of viable male births and the short life span, there was a rather valid argument that there were already too few men available to properly propagate the species, so why lower the odds of survival further by forcing them to kill each other?

In regards to the first, the U.S. was simply outvoted, and the veto power was sold to China in exchange for forgiving its rather massive debt, of which the interest alone was 150 percent of the GDP. (Thank you, Barrack Obama.)

For the second, I'm sure you all know about your mandatory "donations" to the genetic bank.

Now, every decade or so, one young male from every nation is chosen to "participate" in this battle royale. The last man standing wins and as a prize is offered one wish.

If granting this wish is within the power of the ruling council, the Matriarchy, then it will be granted.

If it is not within the counsil's power, he will gain nothing. He will be thrown out onto the streets with only the clothes on his back. Any surviving ladies of his harem will be taken away, unless they insist otherwise.

To date, this has never happened. The winners either wished to live comfortably or remain with their harems for the rest of their lives. Since the lifespan of a teenage male is short, these wishes are happily granted.

(Martufe looks at his notes.) Ah. I must make a correction. There was one wish in the previous tournament that stands out. The winner wished to meet his father. It seems he didn't pay attention during orientation, and missed the part where I mentioned that men DON'T LIVE LONG AFTER PUBERTY. So the wish, while understandable, was impossible, but the letter of the law was applied and the boy was taken to his father's grave.

That's all he got. He was left there, and his harem stayed with him as he grieved. When he died, they went their separate ways and were never heard from again.

From what I can gather, he was buried with his father. There's some sense of closure in that, at least.

Ash Udderweis: "PPPFFFFTTT! Get on with it! This is so boring! Let's just get this game started! I want my prize already!"

Mr. Udderweis (he must come from a LONG line of Swedish cattle ranchers), I don't know how you've been raised, or what you were told before you got here, but in case you haven't noticed, you are going to have to EARN your prize; no one is going to just "give" you anything from this point on. Nothing is guaranteed. Besides, there's no way to know just which "boring" little info I tell you is going to mean the difference between life and death once this game gets started.

(The rest of the class gasps. Martufe stops speaking and takes a moment to look around.)

There are dozens of young men here today. Unfortunately, most of them don't stand a chance, no matter how diligent they are. Shame really, they look quite bright and obedient, perhaps TOO obedient to be effectively independent, let alone leaders. Only good leaders can even make it through the preliminary first round.

There are, however, a few that caught my eye.

First, there's the arrogant jerk who just mouthed off, Ash Udderweis. What I gathered from his file is that he's already had several girls chosen for him, and he bosses them around ruthlessly. They are terrified of him and his wrath. There are the makings of a tyrant with this one.

On the other extreme is this cross-dressing young boy, Alex Dolorean. Surprisingly, he is an only child. Something went wrong during the pregnancy, and his poor mother can't have any more children. Doesn't surprise me in the least that she raised him as a girl to hide him from the prying eyes of the Matriarchy, hoping against hope that she could keep him, at least until she could lay her eyes on some grandchildren.

Sadly, it didn't go that way. The Matriarchy found out, as it always does, and quite literally ripped him from his mother's arms, dragging him here in the middle of the night, and yes, it was a dark and stormy night. It's a minor miracle he's even here now. Several other vehicles driving the same road were not so lucky. Many major accidents took a great deal of lives that night.

It's not surprising that he's quite timid, almost shy, but he's generous and kind, makes friends easily, and since he was raised as a girl, knows quite a few who like him because he treats them right. In other words, he inspires loyalty. In fact, I have received petitions from several of his friends to be his "brides" as opposed to making him choose from the local "pool" of girls despite knowing that they're putting their lives on the line by doing so. Loyalty like that is rare amongst the rare these days, especially towards men, thanks to the constant anti-male propaganda going on.

In fact, that episode of the *"The Outer Limits"* where a guy suddenly finds himself lost and alone in a village full of women raised to believe that men are the embodiment of pure evil is broadcast as a public service announcement (PSA) daily.

Some of the others who stand out are:

Mercedes Overhorn. That is a spoiled brat who really gets on my nerves. If he sees it, he wants it. If he wants it, it's "his" by some bizarre birthright. Obviously, nobody has ever told him "no," or he was raised by having money thrown at him to shut him up.

Arcades Allbright who constantly harps about male superiority.

Kakizaki Ikari is a complete and total thrall to Mr. Allbright.

And lastly, Tendo Akaneda who is a complete mystery except that he has three child-like groupies who just love being in his presence.

Chapter One

SHORTLY AFTER CLASS ended, Mr. Alex Dolorean approached me with some questions. Unbeknownst to either of us, Mr. Ash Udderweis was hiding around the corner, watching with growing jealousy and hatred.

"How dare he? That little punk trying to sneak a favor or two and one-up me?! I'll show him a thing or two. He'll learn to respect the name 'Udderweis' soon enough."

Over the following days, Alex was subjected to "pranks" increasing in frequency and severity. It began simply enough, glue on his school desk, graffiti on his bedroom door, but quickly escalated to break-ins and rampant vandalism in his quarters, finally ending in a horrific beating from ten other "participants" while Ash laughed.

I arrived on the scene and stopped the attack, but what came next was shocking, even to me. The Matriarchy covered for Ash, saying that Alex had merely "fallen down the stairs and the others were helping him up, isn't that right, Mr. Dolorean?" Alex never got to answer the question as he fell unconscious and was taken to the infirmary where he has stayed ever since. Unbelievable! So this was why Ash was so cocky. He'd been getting support from the Matriarchy from the beginning. He thought he was PROMISED the "prize!"

Well, there was no way I was going to let THAT stand. (Kracks knuckles.) Time for Ash to see how it felt on the receiving end.

While I didn't have time to replicate ALL the suffering Alex went through, I did arrange for Ash to have a little "accident" with the stairs. It was so easy, since Ash loved (and still loves) to walk around with his nose up in the air, as if he was superior to everyone. When he reached the bottom, I called the other ten.

"OK everyone. It seems Mr. Udderweis has had a little accident. Strangely, his injuries don't match those worn by Mr. Dolorean. Now, we can't embarrass the Matriarchy. All of you need to 'help him up' in the same way you 'helped' Mr. Dolorean. If Mr. Udderweis doesn't at least have head-to- toe bruising, it has been determined that ALL OF YOU, including Mr. Udderweis, will walk the jungle to the starting point of the game. I must say, that your chances of survival in doing so are very low."

Meanwhile, Alex Dolorean was not idle. He was studying the past games, trying to learn the layout of the field. That's not all. Even though he was bedridden, he was still forging alliances with the locals of the arena, the most vicious beasts in the field, velociraptors and dire wolves.

Some of the beasts came to his window, this wasn't supposed to happen. All sorts of safety measures were in place to make certain dangerous animals didn't get too close to the training center.

I mean, all the screaming, running, bleeding, and dying is supposed to take place on camera for the amusement of the audience (by the way, viewing is mandatory) not off camera during training and orientation.

When he saw them, he didn't cry out in fear, he didn't panic, he didn't try to run or hide. Instead, he welcomed them into the room, shared his food with them, pet them, and laughed and played with them. We didn't find out about this until sometime later when Ash's thralls went to "punish Alex for humiliating them and their 'boss,' Ash."

They smashed their way into his room, with weapons stolen from the training grounds, expecting to find a helpless, bedridden boy. Instead, they came face-to-face with row upon row of razor-sharp teeth and deadly claws, all quite angrily pointing their way.

Needless to say, things didn't go their way. Some lost arms, some lost legs, and some lost eyes, ears, or noses. In short, while seriously wounded, none of them died. Those with life-threatening injuries were treated, the rest were not, at least not to any extent above making sure their injuries didn't become life threatening.

When they complained, I simply told them, "Consider this your punishment for 'jumping the gun.' You all know the fighting is only allowed in THE ARENA, and remember, Alex isn't the one breaking into people's rooms."

When the guards finally arrived at the scene, and they in turn summoned me, Alex hugged one of the raptors and cried out, "They are my friends! Don't hurt them!" Although he had tears in his eyes, he had the look of a warrior like none I'd seen in a long, long time, a look that said, "If you hurt them, I will never forgive you." The beasts were tranquilized and taken back to the jungle after which I gave the guards a severe rebuke.

"How could something like this happen!?! What are raptors and wolves doing in his room? How did they get past the electric fences, barbed wire, etc. designed to keep dangerous animals out?

Furthermore, what the heck were those ten doing with weapons from the combat training center? Those aren't supposed to leave there under any circumstances, and they're to be kept under lock and key!"

Suddenly, one of the guard's radios crackled to life. "Hey! What's the situation? That sissy bite the dust yet?"

Martufe: "So THAT'S what's going on?! This dangerous situation was ignored while you were taking BETS on when our 'guest' was going to die?! Need I remind you, ladies, that the Matriarchy wants the fighting, bleeding, and dying ON CAMERA?"

I assigned two guards at random. "You and you, guard that medical bay 24/7 until Alex is fully recovered or the Games begin. I don't care how you break up the shifts. If you need reinforcements, don't hesitate to ask. Anyone trying to enter there, without my express order, will face EXPULSION from here to the detention facility. I shouldn't have to tell you what that means, although I can say from firsthand experience that it's a fate worse than death."

"As for the rest of you, spread the word. If you guards get 'bored' like this again, there are many, many duties that I would be more than happy to delegate. I can leave the details to your imagination."

At the mention of that, the guard's faces all went pale. They knew full well the "duties" to which I referred, the deadly, dangerous ones. The word indeed does spread quickly. There was no more chatter about "when the sissy is going to 'get it.'"

This would be far from the nastiest trick in store for young, Alex Dolorean. The Matriarchy still had some rather nasty surprises in store for him, starting with the bride selection.

(The scene shifts to the bridal holding area where the future harem brides are selected.)

Normally, Alex, along with the other "contestants," would be summoned to the central plaza where he would be introduced to his bridal candidates. Even though this would occur in the last phase of training and Alex had had plenty of time to recover, his unique situation had confined him to the medical wing, and he could not attend.

The girls were drawn by lots and went through formal "marriage interviews" or, as known in the former nation of Japan, *omiai*, a tradition of "arranged marriage" that lasted until the pandemic was well underway and there simply weren't enough men to go around.

In this case, it was being used as a "market" of sorts where, presumably, contestants choose those with abilities that gave them the best hope of winning or that best suited their personalities. What the girl wanted and felt generally was given no thought since most were indentured to be here either to pay their own debts, the debts of their family, or their debt to society, in other words, criminals sent here as punishment.

I am one of those prospective brides, Shiatsu. Once you get thrown into this mix, your family name no longer matters. It is erased by law. If you're lucky, far luckier than you deserve, you are given the name of the victor, as his (or one of his) surviving brides. Even if he wins, he's under no obligation to give you anything, not even a name. Usually "players" attack each other by going through each other's harems. So if he loses, usually, you're already dead.

How did I get here? Well, it's a real long, sad story, one that I'd rather not dwell on, although the time may come when I'll share it.

Right now, though, my attention is on the prospective "grooms" who will examine me. One by one, the cells around me empty, and when the girls don't return, I know they've been "chosen" by someone. I doubt they'll be treated well. They most certainly aren't being married out of love or even getting a sacred ceremony with the priestess, a white dress, and a walking down the aisle.

As for those girls who are NOT chosen, their fate is far crueler. Those rare few who are seen again, work as slaves. I shudder to think of what happens to the rest. I hope against hope that I am not one of them, seeing as my chances of being chosen dwindle, the fewer of us there are.

Finally, my name is called, and I am brought into the plaza. There was still a slim hope that there were those who took the maximum fifteen brides but that there were still others who hadn't gotten the minimum six yet, and another shipment would be brought in, but that hope was in vain.

All the others have been chosen, and I am the last. All the players, except one, have chosen at least their minimum quota. The one who still needs brides isn't even here! Is this a cruel joke? Am I only being brought in to be officially sentenced to slavery, or worse!?

My fears are soon answered when a member of the Matriarchy appears before me. "Even though Ash Udderweis has asked for you, he already has his allotted quota, fortunately for you."

Ash Udderweis! So HE is a player here? That prick! He's part of the reason I'm in this mess.

"Mercedes Oberhorn also asked for you, but he filled up his quota quickly too. We really can't find any rhyme or reason for his choices except that, like a kid in a candy store, he just grabbed the first pretty things he saw without any thought whatsoever."

That spoiled brat is here too?! Just how many of my former "clients" am I going to be paraded in front of?

"The reason we brought you out, is that we have a bit of a problem. One of the contestants couldn't be here today due to injury, and so he doesn't have his allotment of brides yet."

I take a quick look around, and see some badly crippled boys. The one whom I'm being chosen for must be in a grave state indeed if these guys are here, but he's not.

"He only needs one more to meet the minimum, and we would like you to be that one, but there's a catch."

I knew it! Here it comes. I sigh deeply before asking, "What is it you need me to do?"

"Nothing too special. Just collect a sperm sample."

Flabbergasted, I cry out, "Sperm sample? I'm not a lab tech. I don't have the right tools or training to collect any tissue samples, especially not something that dangerous!"

"Oh, dear, we know all too well about your 'training,' and we've tried the clinical approach, repeatedly, without success. None of the samples we've obtained have been anywhere near viable. We thought a more … DIRECT approach was in order."

So that's it. They want me to get his sperm through SEXUAL means, hoping that what they scrape out of me will provide a viable sample for whatever their agenda is. "Seems like I don't have a choice, do I?"

"Excellent. It's good that we could come to an 'understanding.' We need you to get started right away."

Remembering my weekly "calendar," I start to object, but before I can say anything...

"If you're going to say what we think, then that's all the better. If we can't get a viable sample, we can always examine the offspring. Just remember, we don't need your APPROVAL, only your OBEDI-ENCE."

Knowing full well that my life is in their hands, all I can do is grit my teeth and agree to their inhumane demands. "Where is he now?"

"In the medical wing, Just ask Martufe O'oharra to guide you. There was an 'incident,' and security's been locked down there."

Confused and curious, I seek out Martufe O'oharra, the caretaker of this training center, and tell him about my assignment to Alex Dolorean.

Martufe: "So you're the 'bride' assigned to Alex by the Matriarchy, eh? I'm sure there are strings attached, right?"

Before I can say anything, he says, "Don't worry. I won't pry. It's just that I'm charged with his safety, and if anything more happens to him, there will be consequences."

Shiatsu: "So can I ask what did happen?"

Martufe: "I have no problem answering that question. The 'official' story is that Alex took a fall down some stairs, and went to the medical bay." (whispering) "The truth is that Alex has been targeted by bullies from day one, and a gang of ten boys beat him senseless." (back to normal speech) "But that's not the worst part, the worst part is, those ten boys who 'helped him get up' decided to break into his medical room and finish beating him to death."

Reading the look of horror on my face, he continues, "Don't worry, they got their comeuppance. Seems Mr. Dolorean had a couple of rather nasty surprises waiting for them. Suffice it to say, each and every one of those thugs now knows what it's like to be torn apart by a pack of wild animals. As a result, nobody is allowed entry into Mr. Dolorean's room without my explicit order or consent. The guards are also 'highly motivated' to comply with my orders in this matter."

Good gods, what exactly am I being thrust into?

Before I realize it, we stop in front of Alex's room, the two guards open the door for us, and we step in.

Martufe: "Alex, there's someone here I want you to meet."

Alex: "Hello, Mr. O'oharra. Who is this?"

Martufe: "Shiatsu, this is Alex Dolorean. Alex, this is Shiatsu. I'll leave you two kids alone so you can get to know each other."

Shiatsu: "So what are you doing in bed, kiddo? Did they really hurt you that bad?"

Alex: "Yeah… the nurses don't want these to open up again."

When Alex lifts up his shirt, I count over one hundred stitches across his stomach. WHAT KIND OF BEATING DID HE TAKE?

Shiatsu: "You lived through that? You must be one tough kid."

Alex: "I wish so. Then I wouldn't be stuck in here, and Mommy wouldn't have been taken away. But my friends took care of them for me!"

Shiatsu: "I was told about that. Weren't you afraid?"

Alex: "Nah. MeiFang (My Fang) and Skay Lee (Scaly) would never hurt me."

This kid must be absolutely fearless; he doesn't even have the slightest trepidation concerning the most vicious animals created by genetic engineering.

Now how am I going to seduce him? He obviously isn't "adult" enough for subtlety, but if I just try to jump him, it won't go well at all. Guess I'll have to "ease" him into it. Wouldn't be the first time I've been instructed to "initiate" someone.

Shiatsu: "Wait. You said your mother was taken away?"

Alex: "Yeah. A lot of really mean people with guns came in the middle of the night, shoved my mother into a car, and dragged me here. I'm going to win so I can see her again!"

Sounds like I'm not the only one who's here because the Matriarchy likes kicking doors down in the middle of the night.

Shiatsu: "Don't worry. It'll be OK... somehow." (sniff, sniff). "Whew! What's that smell? Have you been bathing regularly?"

Alex: "Nurses told me not to, at least not the last time they came. They showed me how to clean and prepare the bandages though."

Shiatsu: "Well, you REALLY need a bath, kiddo. Come on, I'll help you."

Alex: "Really? They said it was OK?"

Shiatsu: "I think it will be worse if we don't. You don't want an infection. Trust me."

Alex: "Yeaay! These clothes were getting all smelly and itchy anyway."

He takes off his "hospital gown" with relish. It's a good thing too; it reeks like nobody's business. Underneath, there's cotton gauze wrapped around his chest and back several times.

Shiatsu: "You've got wounds on your chest too?"

Alex: "Eh? Oh you mean this?" (points at the gauze) "That's to hold 'these' down."

Alex carefully unwraps his chest, and while there are no wounds there, aside from plenty of bruises, there's something I never expected to see on a guy, two things actually, and they're bigger than mine!

Shiatsu: "You're a boy, right?"

Alex: "Mommy told me that I'm a girl and said that's what I should tell everyone, but the mean ladies said I'm a boy. I don't know!"

Great! "He" is gender confused too. Oh, I almost forgot.

Shiatsu:"Alex, is there a laundry chute or basket, and a change of clothes? It wouldn't be good to put those stinky things on again after a bath."

Alex: "Yeah, you're right. There's more gauze in the drawer just behind my bed, but I haven't been brought fresh clothes in days. The laundry chute is that big steel 'door' there about a foot from my bed. The one next to my bed is how they send up food and water."

He's been caged up like an animal too. Just how challenging does the Matriarchy want to make this?

Shiatsu: "How big is the bathtub anyway?"

Alex: "No bathtub, but there is a shower. Why? Could it be you want to bathe too?"

Finally! Something is going my way for once. At the very least, it's a good way to "innocently" test his comfort zone.

Shiatsu: "Yeah. It was a long trip here, and I'm kind of sweaty. Would you like to bathe together?"

Alex suddenly beams with... joy?

Alex: "Really!? That would be great! I haven't bathed with someone in a long time! Even though it's just a shower, that would be awesome, though I miss just sitting and talking in the bathtub with someone."

He certainly doesn't LOOK perverted when he's saying this, and it seems like it's not lust but just genuine loneliness.

I am genuinely happy to get out of that drab prison/indentured bride uniform and eagerly throw it and that "gown" he was forced to wear down the laundry chute. Even if it's just a symbolic gesture, it's nice to throw off those trappings that indicate that I've gone from "human" to "property" even for a little while.

Alex: "Oh, you're so lucky!"

Shiatsu: "Eh?"

Alex: "You don't need a giant gauze bandage on your chest all the time! I hate these things!"

Just as I'm about to retort, I get a good look at Alex. He's lucky not to have broken bones. Just a mere inspection of his legs, arms, and neck makes me shudder.

My worst days on the street were nothing like that, but what's more interesting is what's BETWEEN his legs. Yes, he's a boy, all right. He's got all the right "equipment," and I would know. He's also well endowed "down there." This explains a lot.

He suddenly notices me looking at his chest, then his crotch, then back to his chest again.

Alex: "What are you looking at?"

I can feel the heat rising to my face. I must be blushing like crazy right now.

Shiatsu: "Err... um... I'm trying to think of how to wash you without hurting your... wounds.."

Alex: "You're worried about my 'thing,' right? I'm not stupid. I've bathed with girls before, and it always weirds them out the first time."

What uncanny instincts. He read me like a book, but not in the way I imagined. Here I am trying to figure out how to start something, and he's trying to reassure me that he won't. Wait, he mentioned bathing with girls before?!

Shiatsu: "Wait, you bathe with girls regularly?"

Alex looks at me like he's confused about something.

Alex: "Yeah. My childhood friends and I would love to wash each other's hair and back, laugh, splash each other, and often just sit and talk. What? Is that something weird?"

Oh! So it's "just bathing" for him. I resist the urge to pinch his cheeks, but do start to chuckle a bit.

Shiatsu:"Oh, that's so cute! Keep thinking like that. Most people don't, and it's sad."

He looks at me like I've got two heads for a moment, then shrugs and turns on the water.

Alex: "Shall we get started then? I don't know about you, but I'm getting kind of itchy."

Shiatsu: "Yes, let's start. Whose back should we wash first?"

Oh, how naïve I was. It never occurred to me that we were being watched, and that the room was wired for sound. Martufe and the Matriarchy saw and heard everything. Martufe, at least, can justify it by the fact that both vicious animals AND armed thugs came into this room. The Matriarchy, however, only had prurient interests in mind. In blissful ignorance of the Matriarchy's growing voyeuristic impatience, I took my time in making Alex comfortable with my presence.

We laughed, played with the shower head, and washed each other's hair. He was, and still is, fascinated by my naturally silver hair.

While washing each other's bodies, I had plenty of time to examine him, in detail. Yep, those breasts are real. I know implants when I feel them. He also has something else that belongs to women. He's a true hermaphrodite. No wonder the Matriarchy wants a sperm sample so badly.

Still blissfully unaware of the surveillance, after the bath, we head back to the patient's' area and I finally "get to work." Choosing a "fresh" bed, I begin to passionately kiss him. Surprisingly, his eyes become glassy and he immediately loses all resistance. The whole time we're making love, I get the eerie feeling that he's not as virginal as he appears. He's just too damn good! It's like he can read my body better than I can. I think, "If only he would...," and seconds later, he's doing it! Whether it's cupping my breasts, nibbling on my ear, lightly pinching my nipple(s), or anything else, even running his fingers through my hair, he does it! Wave after wave of pleasure overcomes me.

After we're finished though, looking into his eyes, it's like he just woke up and realized what we did, and his face is a mask of terror, sheer unrelenting terror. That is NOT a look I expected to see. It gets worse. One of the Matriarchy, with her personal goon squad, smashes her way into the room immediately after we've completed our love making, grabs me off the bed, and slaps me into the stirrups! They're going to take the sample forcefully, even though I agreed to give it to them before!

Alex: "NO! Don't hurt her! Let her go!"

Goon 1: "Settle down, kid. This doesn't concern you."

Alex: "I SAID LET HER GO!"

Suddenly, before my eyes, the goon is sent flying out of the room by a large metal spike coming out the back of his hand, and while retracting it, he cuts the matriarch's face.

Turning parts of my body into blades is MY power! How did he do that?

"You dare cut my face, You BRAT!"

She tasers him with a flick of her hand.

Paralyzed and unable to move, he is forced to watch as I am poked, prodded, and his sperm is roughly removed from inside me. I can't even begin to describe the pain and humiliation. She doesn't even spend any time lubricating the tools. "Allright. We're done here." She then points at Alex and says, "I will see you die horribly, in the arena."

I'm unceremoniously dumped onto the tile floor, along with a change of clothes for myself and Alex, and left to cry with him.

Alex: "Never again."

Shiatsu: "Hmm?"

Alex: "I will never be weak again!"

Shiatsu: "Shh. It's OK! You sent the goon flying, and you cut her up pretty good. That's better than I could have done."

Alex: "You're my bride, aren't you?"

Shiatsu: "That's right."

Alex: "Damn it! Less than a week left, and I haven't even finished healing yet! I also missed the 'choosing ceremony!' I don't even have the minimum six brides!"

Martufe: "Oh, don't worry. You've got five others coming. They should be here tomorrow morning. You know them well. I must say, you're going to have a powerful team there. Get some rest tonight. Your training starts tomorrow, and you've got plenty of catching up to do."

Shiatsu: "And what brings you here?"

Martufe just smirks, "Couldn't help notice this 'girl' here getting thrown out of the room." He picks up the unconscious personal guard of the matriarch and then takes on a more serious tone. "I would have stopped them if I could. The Matriarchy's behavior is completely inexcusable. Get dressed. We're moving you, both of you, to new quarters. This room is not secure. Not in the slightest. By the way, was this YOUR doing?"

Shiatsu: "No. It was his, though I don't understand how."

Martufe: "BWAHAHAHAHA! Being beaten unconscious by a guy in a hospital bed with over one hundred stitches in his gut? Oh she is NEVER going to live that down."

I allow myself a meek smile. "In one blow no less."

I, Alex Dolorean, aside from collecting my notes on the arena, didn't even put on the gauze tape to tie down my breasts as I usually do. Shiatsu advised against it, and seeing that she has way more medical experience than I do, and says that they'll heal better when they're not taped down, I reluctantly have to agree. I still don't like it though. Those things jiggle, bounce, and shake in all sorts of distracting ways.

Chapter Two

TRUE TO MARTUFE'S word, we are moved from the medical clinic to the "harem suite." Fortunately, the move was quick since our only possessions right now are the clothes on our bodies, and some sheets of paper (as well as the room itself; though, it makes my initial room and the medical room I was staying in look like a pair of closets by comparison. Two large queen-size beds, a sauna and a claw-footed bathtub, a six-pack dresser drawer, and a closet big enough to be a room all by itself, with as well as a mirrored ceiling as well are all found here. Seven people could easily live here quite comfortably. There's no dumb waiter here though, so I guess it's going to be a common cafeteria for everyone.)

Shiatsu: "Want to try the sauna?"

She must see something on my face because before I can say anything, she says, "No, we are not going to do 'that.' The last thing we need is to give the matriarch's goon squad a reason for storming in here."

She looks annoyed after an involuntary sigh of relief escapes my lips. Sorry, Shiatsu, but "that" scares me! I just can't separate "that" and the "contribution" the Matriarchy got from me before I got here in my mind. As if watching my mother being shoved into a car and taken away wasn't enough, they took me to a holding center with a bunch of "boys" and told me repeatedly that's what I am. Then, when they saw "these" (starts massaging breasts), they immediately separated me from everyone else, put me in a dark room, and after that showed me a bunch of naked girls doing strange things with "men." When that didn't cause any reaction other than confusion, they got some bizarre machine and attached it to that thing between my legs and forced me to watch that stuff over and over again while the machine did weird things to me.

Shiatsu: "Anyway. I just figured that soaking in the tub would help us relax, and help your wounds heal."

Alex: "Yeah. That sounds good to me. Where do we put our clothes?"

Shiatsu: "Let's just fold them and put them in the dresser, for now. We only have the one outfit, so let's treat it right, OK?"

I have to admit, she was right. Soaking in the sauna did worlds of good for both of us. The dull aches everywhere finally calmed down, and she was VERY visibly relaxed. Getting to sleep after the sauna was easy. We didn't even bother to put our clothes back on. We just lay down, pulled the sheets up, and at least I was out like a light.

The sleep was not peaceful though, not for me. All night long, I had horrible nightmares in which I was running down dark alleys, being chased by strange shapeless beings, and fighting wave after wave of faceless people who were trying to kill me, rob me, or hurt me, badly. I must have been crying out in my sleep, because the next morning, the first thing I saw was Shiatsu looking into my face, patting my head gently, and saying "Did you know you cry out in your sleep?" The wet spots under my eyes confirmed it. Furthermore, something else she said really shocked me awake. "You REALLY love my breasts, don't you?" Sure enough, I was in a VERY compromising position, lips on one breast, hand on the other. I thought she'd be angry, but instead she just kissed me lightly on the forehead, and said, "Let's get dressed. Breakfast is going to start soon, and I'd rather we didn't miss it, even if we're going to be surrounded by a bunch of jerks. On the bright side, we're going to meet those new brides of yours. We need all the help we can get."

On the way to breakfast, I told Shiatsu about the dreams I had. She turned to look at me with a look that's not easy to put into words. It was a mix of annoyance, possibly anger, fear, worry, and no small part surprise. "Those sound VERY familiar to me. I LIVED those. Where did you get that imagery?" When I honestly told her that I didn't know, she turned a disbelieving eye to me, and said, "You've got no reason to lie to me. So I'll believe you, for now. The coincidence is just too startling for words, although all MY dreams centered on SOMEONE sucking my breast while crying, 'Mommy.'"

Shiatsu was right; waiting for us at the cafeteria, was a crowd giving us death glares. Martufe was also right. My other five brides were there too, and I did indeed know them! I've known them almost all my life! I had absolutely no problem recognizing them.

Alex: "What are you guys doing here?! Do you know you could get killed just being here?"

Shiatsu: "Before you start upbraiding them, could you at least introduce us?"

Alex: "Ah, sorry. Guys, meet Shiatsu, the first bride assigned to me. Shiatsu, meet my childhood friends whom I've known most of my life."

"The red-haired one with black eyes is Atari. She's got a bit of a fiery temper."

"The one with blue hair and blue eyes is Sega. Like the ocean, she can be perfectly calm one moment and dangerously fierce the next without any warning."

"The brunette with hazel eyes is Sierra. She's as solid as a rock, but if you cross her, she'll come down on you like a ton of bricks or a landslide."

"The golden-haired beauty with golden eyes is Diana. Her entrance is like a breath of fresh air, but when she's vexed, she will blow you away."

When I get to the bronze‑ haired girl with brown eyes, "The fifth and final member is, Shinobi. She…"

Shiatsu and Shinobi: "We've met."

Alex: "You two know each other?"

Atari: "Why didn't you mention your friend sooner?"

Shinobi: "She's no friend."

Shiatsu: "Likewise. The rest of you seem like 'good boys and girls,' so how do you know HER?"

Alex: "What's this about?"

Shiatsu: "We are, or at least were, members of rival 'unions,' right, Shinobi?"

Shinobi: "I have no obligation to answer you. Besides, discussing our past HERE would be… unwise, too many eyes and ears, if you get my meaning."

Shiatsu: "For the moment, I must agree. Eventually, though, we WILL hash this out."

The discussion is suddenly stopped as an announcement comes over the intercom.

Martufe: "Due to several security breaches, all your rooms have been searched, and your possessions confiscated. Before you complain, this is by the order of the Matriarchy. When you're done with your breakfast, you will all return to your rooms where a wardrobe has been provided. You will exchange the clothes you are wearing now for three outfits per person. Aside from the official training garb in the gym, these are the only outfits you will wear during the duration of the Games, so choose wisely."

Alex: "I guess it was wise to keep 'these' with me at all times, after all."

I distribute my notes concerning the arena amongst the girls. Shiatsu's gorgeous purple eyes go wide with wonder. The others aren't far behind.

Shiatsu: "When and where did you get these?"

Alex: "Did you think I spent my hospital visit watching cartoons and playing video games?"

Everyone: "Hospital visit?!"

Noticing the death glares from my assailants, I state, "You'll hear all about it when we choose our new outfits."

We then proceed to eat our humble breakfast of instant or powdered/ reprocessed food in silence.

When we get to our room at the harem suite, we find that Martufe's story was a huge understatement. If I hadn't taken my notes with me, they would surely have been seized. The entire room was obviously searched and put back together in haste. Right in the center, though, is a rather large collection of clothes, of all shapes, sizes, and fashions. Suddenly, the girls get this gleam in their eyes that I know all too well.

"TIME TO PLAY DRESS UP!"

Alex: "No! It's too embarrassing! Didn't you get enough times with dolls growing up?!"

Diana: "Oh, no! Dolls can't fidget embarrassed like you! That's where the fun is! Oh, and we have a new player too!"

Everyone begins looking at Shiatsu.

Atari gropes her from behind. "Eh? What's this? An A cup? Less? How disappointing."

Atari then proceeds to remove my shirt forcefully, "Hey, careful."

Atari: "Oh, relax. There's nothing we haven't seen before...."

The girls recoil in both shock and horror. "WHAT HAPPENED THERE?!" (pointing at my stomach) "And where did you get THOSE?!" Sega starts poking my breasts.

Alex: "Ow! Stop it, please. They still hurt."

Shiatsu: "Are these the friends you bathed with regularly?"

Alex: "Until I was ten, yes. They just stopped one day, and I don't know why."

Shinobi: "I didn't stop. It was his mother's idea, though we never actually 'did anything.' I can say, he's had 'those' for quite a while. The abdomen/stomach wound is new though."

I proceed to tell them the story of the pranks, the bullying, and the eventual beating. Needless to say, they are not amused.

Atari: "Where are they?! I'll roast them alive!"

Sega: "They really need to soak their heads for a while, like until they stop breathing, perhaps?"

Diana: "Oh, you want them to stop breathing? I'll just suck the air out of their lungs!"

Sierra: "Speaking of air, I don't need to tear up the ground. I can pull the dust right out of the air and turn it to stone."

Shinobi: "They'll never see it coming."

I then tell them the story of how they tried to break into the hospital room and met their comeuppance. "They've been punished here, but who knows what they'll try in the arena."

Shiatsu: "It's probably better to plan for each of them having the full set. That's 160 opponents."

Alex: "176. Don't forget the ring leader, Ash Udderweis. Even though he looks like the kind of guy who holds back while others do the fighting, there's no telling what he'll do."

Shiatsu: "Correct. I can confirm that Ash has the maximum fifteen. The Matriarchy made a point of telling me when I got here."

Alex: "Why would they do that?"

Shiatsu: "Ash and I have a 'history.' That's all I feel comfortable saying right now."

Shinobi nods her head. "As do I. The guy is bad news."

Shiatsu: "There's someone else here that has a history with us, Shinobi, Mercedes Oberhorn."

Shinobi: "Th...that spoiled brat is here too? I thought his 'mommy dearest' would 'persuade' the Matriarchy to keep him out of the Games! Guy thinks anything he sees is his! I'm just glad Alex's mother bought my indenture contract and not him."

Shiatsu: "He's got the max fifteen too, so that's 192 opponents that we can effectively count on."

Everyone: "Hmm. You're right. We have a long week of training ahead of us, but that doesn't let you two off the hook..." Snickering ensues.

After being humiliatingly shuffled around through a bunch of outfit combinations, they all settle on three outfits for Shiatsu and me.

The first set is for formal occasions. I wind up wearing a wedding dress with all the trimmings, a gorgeous veil, a flowing train, white sandals with elevated heels, elbow-length white gloves, and thigh-high white socks.

Shiatsu winds up wearing the standard tux with cummerbund, white dress gloves, bow tie, and highly polished dress shoes with a brass buckle.

Everyone: "CUUUTTTEEE!!! Too bad we can't take a picture!"

Alex: "Well. If these games are like all the others, the final night of 'training' will end with a formal party and picture shoot."

Everyone gets stars in their eyes. "SQUEE!!"

Shiatsu: "Why am I wearing the tux?"

Shinobi: "Not to be too blunt, but none of these outfits match your 'body type,' dear, especially in the chest."

Alex (nervously) : "I like her chest. That tux looks lovely.! It really fits well. You're so lucky!"

Shiatsu: "W... well, if you say so." (blushes furiously.)

Atari: "Oooh! Someone's cheeks are going to bruise!"

The rest of them look like bride's maids. Atari is dressed in a flaming red dress with some kind of ruby decorations. Sega's dress is pure aqua ordained with sapphires. Sierra's gown is velvet-green with emeralds. Diana's dress is the color of desert sand, ruffled to look like dunes, and embroidered with sunflowers and dandelion seeds.

Alex: "Wow! You girls are pretty, very pretty! It's like a painting come to life!"

Everyone: "Flattery will get you... DRESSED UP!"

Before they can go any further, the locked door opens, and there's the matriarch with her armed squad in tow.

Matriarch: "Good job last night, Shiatsu. Unfortunately, the sample was negative. We'll have to go with Plan B. I'm glad you are all so 'intimate' with each other. It should be easy to get a nice variety of specimens. Oh, that IS a nice look you have there, 'boy.' It should get all the tongues wagging. See you in the arena. Hohohoho!" Then she leaves.

Shiatsu runs, shuts, and locks the door.

Everyone: "What was THAT about?!"

Alex: "That... BITCH! What she did last night wasn't enough?!"

While I, Shiatsu, can't blame him for the sentiment, the other girls are aghast. This must be the first time EVER he's uttered that phrase.

Sega: "I don't believe it. No matter how badly he was treated, Alex never used... THAT WORD. Not ever."

Shinobi: "Shiatsu, you have some explaining to do. Why would the Matriarch say 'good work' to you?"

Alex: "Last night, that... 'woman,' she... she..." Tears start flowing freely.

I put my index finger on his lips to silence him, kiss his forehead gently, and say, "Alex, what I have to say next is something you shouldn't hear. Go into the closet, shut the door, and cover your ears until I come get you, OK? I would tell you to wait outside, but that's not safe, not anywhere near so."

Everyone agrees with me on that. After Alex goes into the closet and shuts the door, I tell them exactly how the matriarch ordered me to get his "sample" or else I would be sent to the "exile camp" as a "rejected maiden" and how both Ash Udderweis and Mercedes Oberhorn were asking for me.

Most do not understand what that means, but Shinobi happily fills in the blanks.

Shinobi: "The exile camp is a harsh, harsh place. You know about 'debtor's prison,' right?"

Everyone nods.

Shinobi: "The exile camp is far worse. It's a place where those with debts too big to pay in their lifetimes go, or those maidens who are rejected as 'brides' in the Harem Games. Once there, you basically become a slave, sold to the highest bidder, if you're lucky."

While I know that to be true, the others all gasp.

Shinobi: "I was there, as a career criminal. Shiatsu knows my past, and I, hers. We were in rival gangs, after all. Day after day, I watched my old gang disappear one by one. When my turn came, I figured I was doomed. Instead I was luckier than I had any right to be. At age ten, I was bought by Ms. Dolorean, Alex's mother, and met five of the most wonderful women in the world. Further, I met Alex himself. The closest thing to being lecherous was bathing with him, at his mother's request. I can only guess that she wanted something to develop between us, but it never did. He never had any lustful desires towards me, nor did he try to take advantage. He saw me as a friend, maybe even a sister, and treated me as a person, not as property. He wanted me to be happy, above everything else, without asking anything in return. He is the first person who EVER did that for me. I will always love him for it."

Atari taps her back gently.

Shinobi: "To my eternal shame, I ran and hid the night 'they' came to our house and took my master and mistress away." She starts crying.

Sega: "It's all right, dear. If you had stayed, or even fought, you would have been captured, killed, or sent to exile camp and wouldn't be here to help now. He wouldn't have the minimum number of 'brides' for the Games."

Shinobi: "(sob) "OK, I've finished my story. Now please finish yours, Shiatsu. I would not wish being bought by Ash Udderweis or Mercedes Oberhorn upon my worst enemy."

I then proceed to tell everyone how after I "seduced" Alex, the matriarch and her goon squad literally smashed their way into the medical room, roughly grabbed me and scraped my insides for their precious "sample" while Alex was forced to watch. Everyone's mood immediately turns very dark.

Shinobi : "She's a dead woman walking."

Sierra: "But what did she mean by 'specimens?'"

Shiatsu: "Yesterday was 'my special day of the week.' I'm sure you can figure out the rest."

Atari: "You mean she wants our… our… our….!"

Shiatsu: "Oh, absolutely. She made that QUITE clear to me before-hand."

Alex breaks out of the closet and comes rushing up to me, hugging me tightly, face in my chest, crying.

Alex: "NO! She can't have them! She will NEVER have them! I'm sorry, really sorry. I tried not to hear you, I really did! I just couldn't help it!"

Everyone: "So he still does 'that,' eh?"

Shiatsu: "Wait, he did 'that' with you too?"

Shinobi: "Yeah, creeped me out a bit, but his mother told me it's a sub-conscious behavior he picked up when he was really small, and he only does it when he's EXTREMELY stressed out. She was hoping he'd outgrow it eventually. Doesn't seem like that's going to happen soon."

Sega: "If he WASN'T stressed out after everything that's happened, and what he just heard, I'd be worried."

Diana: "Honey, doesn't matter the circumstances. You're his first. You always will be. That has a special place in his heart. It will not change, no matter what happens. We were hoping it would be one of us, but what's done is done. Alex, just... don't neglect us, OK?"

Sierra: "Yeah. If what that bitch meant what she said, she's going to find a way to make sure we 'get some.'"

Shiatsu: "Oh, I forgot to mention, she also said they tried getting samples, clincally, and failed too."

Alex: "You mean those machines that do weird things to you and those strange books?"

Atari: "So they abused the machines made by my mother's company? Oh, Alex!"

Atari: "This is very disturbing news."

Diana: "What do you mean?"

Atari: "We all know how the world is mostly women, right?"

Everyone nods.

Atari : "Well, women still want sex, right? Bu other women alone won't do, right?"

Suddenly revelation starts spreading across everyone's face, but Alex's.

Atari: "Well, my mom's company makes machines that faithfully replicate EVERY aspect of sexual activity for women who want a man but can't get one. If the Matriarchy retooled, and reprogrammed those machines to use on men, against their consent,...poor Alex, you've been violated, repeatedly, you and Shiatsu both. "

Sierra: "We will NEVER understand how that feels, since it has never happened to us, nor do we want it to."

Shinobi: "It would not surprise me if this isn't just about 'specimens' but also making Alex terrified of us."

I suddenly remember the look of terror across Alex's face just before the matriarch broke the door down. "You don't suppose…"

Everyone: "What?!"

Shiatsu: "Never mind. It was just a random thought, one that isn't complete yet, and has no evidence."

Shinobi: "You were going to say that 'Alex is scared of sex,' right?"

Shiatsu: "I never could keep secrets from you. Yes, that IS what crossed my mind."

Alex: "Please stop. You're scaring me!" (snuggles into Shiatsu tighter.)

Yes, he's definitely afraid. It's probably the ONLY thing he fears, yet why is he clinging to me? I'm the one who had sex with him. You think he'd be scared of me too, but he isn't.

Shiatsu: "OK. We'll stop talking about it, right? There's nothing we can do about that right now anyway."

Everyone agrees, and we go back to choosing outfits, but the flurry of activity and the joy in everyone's face is gone, only to be replaced with a grim determination, and no shortage of grief and regret.

In the end, we choose matching leather jerkins for the arena for all of us in camouflage style. We feel it's the most adaptable outfit type for any situation.

For the last choice, we decide to wear pajama-type outfits for sleeping, as opposed to having backup clothing for the arena. Even though Alex and I have already slept together naked, and the others don't seem to have a problem with the concept, we figure it's better if we're prepared to leave the room in a hurry should the need arise in the middle of the night. Considering everything that's happened so far, it's not an unreasonable precaution.

I get a silver-colored pajama outfit to match my hair. Alex gets a purple outfit that matches my eyes. "It's my favorite color," he says, and everyone else nods. I only now notice that his hair is also a wonderful shade of indigo, and he has silver eyes (coincidence?). The rest get colors that match their "formal" outfits, except that Sierra's pajamas are muted earth tones as opposed to emerald colored.

Once the outfit selections are finalized and made official (the rest are taken away by a robotic servant), we make our way to the training grounds. Anyone who dares to glare at us now, gets glared back twice as hard. The intensity is so harsh that all challengers back down immediately. We move in oval formation with Alex in the center. This is for two reasons.

First, it lets all challengers know that anyone who wants to get at Alex has to go through us.

Second, it sends the message that Alex is in charge, not them. It's "no more Mr. Nice Guy" time.

When we finally get to the training center doors, we meet none other than Ash Udderweis. Much as I would love to pound that arrogant smile off his face, this is Alex's time to rise or fall.

Chapter Three

ASH: "WELL, LOOK what we have here. The little girly man came to play warrior?"

Alex: "That's an interesting question coming from someone who hides in a corner while other guys fight for him ten to one against somebody."

Ash: "You little snot! Don't you dare try to humiliate me! Do you know who you're dealing with?"

Alex: "Oh, I wouldn't dream of trying to humiliate you. You're doing a much better job of it yourself, Ash Udderweis. Perhaps one day you'll graduate from 'hiding in a corner' or 'sending goons to attack an invalid' to 'taking candy from babies?'"

When Ash grabs Alex by the neck, I immediately put a sword to his waist. "Perhaps you'd like to know how it feels to need one hundred stitches in your gut?"

Ash: "So you're going to let your whores do your fighting for you?"

Alex grabs Ash's hand, the one going for his throat, at the wrist and squeezes, hard. A loud cracking sound can be heard.

Ash: "Yaaarrgghh!!"

Alex then proceeds to slap Ash with his own hand, knocking him to the ground.

Ash: "You hit me! You actually HIT… ME!"

Alex: "They are not my 'whores.' They are my BRIDES! I would thank you to remember that."

Ash: "You are dead! Without Martufe protecting you, YOU ARE DEAD!"

Alex: "That is always a possibility. You should remember that the Matriarchy won't be able to cover for you either, and you'll be facing plenty of people AND things that want to do more than just hit you."

Suddenly the matriarch "supervisor" comes our way. "You DARE slander the Matriarchy, Mr. Dolorean, by saying we're playing favorites?!"

Alex: "Not at all. I never said anything of the sort. I merely pointed out that you would be unable to do so, IN THE FUTURE, since he seems to have the impression that he's 'protected' somehow. That is hardly a slanderous statement. Or am I wrong? ARE there plans to rig the Games in Mr. Udderweis's favor? That would be VERY unpopular. The gamblers who bet on the Games won't like it. The bookies who manage the bets won't like it. Certainly the most devout followers of 'the Goddess' won't like someone, even the 'holy Matriarchy,' desecrating the Games.

Even the 'sponsors' who pay exorbitant fees for 'gifts' handed to the contestants, which if I'm not mistaken are a rather large part of your budget, would really hate to see one or more of the contestants being given an unfair advantage."

The matriarch slaps Alex right across the mouth. "Watch your mouth, you little brat. Don't you dare to threaten or talk down to us."

Alex signals us to stop and shakes his head, indicating this isn't the time.

Alex: "With all due respect, that was merely an innocent question. I have no control over how you interpret it. As for the rest, those would be the consequences IF there is even the PERCEPTION of tampering with the Games."

Martufe walks in, clapping. "Well said, Mr. Dolorean. Well said indeed. Matriarch, it is only because of my respect for your office that I've allowed your behavior and the behavior of your subordinates, but this ends now."

Martufe: "It is a verifiable FACT that you have indeed shown prejudice against Alex Dolorean, if not outright favoritism towards Ash Udderweis. As an example, just now you assaulted Mr. Dolorean for simply answering your questions. Furthermore, you are also on record for assaulting and violating one of his brides while he was in the infirmary, as well as property damage to the facilities and armed invasion of said infirmary against which Alex had every right to defend himself. And, let's not forget the incident that put him IN the infirmary in the first place. I was present as you tried to intimidate him into voicing testimony contrary to the facts of him being assaulted by ten others."

Matriarch: "How, ...how dare you...!"

Martufe: "Oh sure, you can arrest me, you can try to 'silence' me, you can put me in a cell somewhere, but I ALWAYS come back, and get my vengeance. Remember that before you say anything else."

The matriarch begins to shudder with rage and indignation.

Martufe: "From now on, if ANYTHING happens to Mr. Dolorean while in my facility, I will hold YOU responsible. He chokes on a chicken wing in the cafeteria, your fault. He slips on a bar of soap in the shower, your fault. A METEOR crashes into his room, your fault. That goes DOUBLE for you, Mr. Udderweis. Should that happen, I will expel Mr. Udderweis to the camp of exiles, under the power of discretion assigned to me, and I will release to the world the surveillance footage, both audio and video, of everything I've just mentioned that clearly implicates you."

Martufe leans over and looks at Alex's face. "Hmm, nothing broken, and no permanent damage. Good. Now this doesn't mean you can go picking fights, OK? But it DOES mean that Madame Matriarch won't be able to just barge into your room any more. I don't know how she was raised, but even the lowliest peasant amongst us knows how to knock when we encounter a locked door."

The matriarch storms off in a rage, screaming, "This is not over!"

Ash Udderweis does the same. "I don't need to train against a weakling like you."

Martufe: "He-hee! I've been wanting to put them in their place for some time. Now get to training, kiddo. You're going to need it. He is right about one thing. Once you get into the arena, I won't be able to help or guide you anymore and 'anything goes.'"

We enter the training room. With it being our appointed time, there is no one else present, although we all know the room is being watched and that guards will rush in if anything happens. We are required to change into the proper training gear and use the provided mock weapons. I choose a wooden broadsword, broadswords being my weapon of choice on the streets. Shinobi, of course, chooses throwing knives, blunted and wooden. I don't know how the others are going to train their powers since I don't see anything resembling a weapon or tool that would allow them to channel their elemental abilities.

I choose to ignore that particular problem for the moment and focus on Alex. He's the one we need to keep alive, after all. It would be best if he could do something to help in the fight. He chooses twin short swords, again wooden practice weapons.

Shiatsu: "OK, Alex. I've been meaning to ask about that blade you used in the infirmary. Have you ever done anything like that before?"

Alex: "No. It just … came to me. I was so ANGRY, I just wanted to push that goon away…"

Shiatsu: "I see, so you just 'awakened.' Hmm. This could be a problem in the arena. Let's see if you've got any basic skills. These may be practice weapons, but it will still hurt if I hit you, so be prepared."

Alex nods and then takes on a near-perfect, twin sword stance. As I circle, he does the same, keeping his distance, watching for any openings in my defense, noting if I see any in his. So I decide to try a simple charge. He blocks it aside with ease using one sword and brings the other to my neck. "Bang! You're dead."

Shiatsu: "Not bad. Seems you've got some training after all."

So I decide to try something a bit more advanced, and he counters it easily. Every time he counters, I increase the difficulty, and every time I increase the difficulty, he increases the finesse of his counter. Finally, I get into moves it took me years of hard fighting to learn, and he STILL counters them, although clumsily. He recovers from his slight mistakes easily. It's like he knows the move in his mind, but his body is simply not used to it.

Shiatsu: "WHO trained you?! Those are moves it took me years on the streets to learn! On the streets, you make a mistake and you're dead, or wishing you were."

Alex: "I wasn't. I never had a 'master.' I just saw you coming, and kind of 'remembered' it."

Shiatsu: "Remembered? No way, the nightmares? That's not possible! There's more going on than you're telling me. I'll get the truth out of you, yet!"

Alex: "Look out!"

Suddenly Alex grabs me aside, swats a throwing knife aimed at the back of my head, and throws the sword he used back at Shiobi.

Suddenly Diana shrieks "Aiee!" and blocks the sword with a wall of air after Shinobi jumps aside.

Shinobi: "I've often told you to be a bit more aware of your surroundings, Shiatsu. If this was our time back on the streets, you'd be dead. Alex, that was impressive. A bit clumsy, seeing as you almost hit Diana there, but if I was just a little less alert, it would have left me a mark to remember."

Shiatsu: "YOU have been training him!?!"

Shinobi: "Well, we loved to play 'tag' while I lived with him, and I used that to keep my skills sharp, but I never actually 'trained' him, nor did anyone else, and you say he had nightmares?"

Alex then goes on to explain how he had visions of fighting in the streets, of being constantly chased, last night.

Shinobi: "I see. He's empathic, with excellent instinctive image training."

Shiatsu: "Image training?"

Shinobi: "Oh, yes. There are martial artists who can learn a move simply by watching it, or imagining it. It is unusual that he would pick up on your memories though, unless he's latently telepathic. We're going to have to see what happens with each of us taking turns in bed with him."

Shiatsu: "YOU have got to be kidding! You want to give the matriarch what she wants?! Not to mention his known trauma.?!"

Shinobi: "Oh, jeez! I meant to sleep! Although..."

She gets real close and whispers in my ear, "Perhaps it's best if we eliminate all extraneous variables? Tonight is 'my special night.' I can't speak for the others though."

When I blush, everyone immediately knows what she whispered. "Hahaha! You are SO easy to read."

Shiatsu: "WHY YOU!..."

Alex: "Um... I have an idea."

Everyone: "Eh?!"

Alex uses the intercom button to contact Martufe. "Excuse me?"

Martufe: "Yes, Alex. Is everything all right?"

Alex: "Yes. I have a question. About the training weapons, is it all right if they get damaged or broken?"

Martufe: "Oh yes, they are cheap, mass produced. We have plenty and can easily make more if need be. Why?"

Alex: "I know this line is not secure, so I'm going to say we've got a training regiment in mind that might be a bit rough on them, and probably the training room."

Martufe: "Oh! The training room is quite sturdy. Knock yourselves out."

Alex: "Thanks."

After shutting off the intercom, he turns to us and says, "OK, everyone. How about a special game of 'soccer?'"

Seeing the perplexed look on everyone's faces, he continues. "It occurred to me when Diana blocked that sword with her wind powers. I figured why not have everyone try to block, deflect, or reflect thrown objects without touching them? Shinobi could pitch, and anyone getting hit by a weapon will be 'out.' The game will end when all but one of us is "out" or the time for training ends, whichever comes first. If we all get 'out' but there's still time remaining, we should start again.

Ideally, we want to get through the entire training time without any of us getting "out," especially Shinobi. As our projectile/ missile weapon specialist, she will need to watch out for those weapons too. Sound like a good idea?"

Shiatsu: "Hmm, now that's clever. I like it."

Shinobi: "Hmm, not bad, and you really wouldn't have to worry about your wound."

Everyone nods in understanding. "Sounds like fun. Let's get started."

Shinobi gathers the throwing knives and immediately makes us all "out."

We keep trying until we finally figure out a rhythm, and the sparks really start to fly. We don't even notice when the training time ends until the next trainees ring the door to come in. They come in with eyes and mouths wide open in surprise. It's quite obvious that the training room got a good workout. There are marks left by elemental attacks everywhere, along with thrown knives in various states of damage and destruction.

Alex: "Sorry about the room. We didn't mean to be so rough, but we did ask and got permission first. So if you guys want to really let loose, it should be OK."

After leaving the room, we hear some stomachs growl. "Hmm, how about we grab some lunch before heading back to our room?"

Shinobi: "Sure, but there's something I've got to speak about with Shiatsu, privately. Could you go ahead?"

Alex: "OK, but don't get too far behind. It's dangerous to be alone."

As soon as we are out of earshot of the others, Shinobi pulls me close and tells me with tears in her eyes, "I was serious in there. I WANT him. It's not fair that I spent years trying to get close to him, playing with him, laughing and crying with him, sharing a bath and a bed with him, and YOU get him first! I know you didn't have a choice, but... bwaaaahhhh!!!"

I never thought I would feel this way towards a bitter, and deadly rival, but I REALLY feel sorry for her. Contrary to my normal instincts, I hug her tightly and pat her head. "Shh. It's all right. You really want his baby?"

Shinobi: (sniff) "Yeah."

Shiatsu: "All right. We're on the same team now. If you REALLY want him, we'll figure something out. You do know we're going to be watched no matter what, right?"

Shinobi: (nods) "Yeah. But, I'm at my limit. I just can't take it anymore."

Shiatsu: "All right. Let's catch up to the others; we don't want someone else catching us."

Unfortunately, that's exactly what happens. The two contestants we LEAST wanted to meet were lying in wait for us. Ash Udderweis confronted us first. "Well, what do we have here? Alex's two little whores got separated from the pack? I'll have you pay for my embarrassment today. Now let's see. What shall we do first?" Outnumbered fifteen to two, we really didn't have much of a chance, but on the streets we've faced worse odds and we're still here. No way we're going to back down from this wannabe.

Mercedes: "Now, now. I don't much care about what happens to Shinobi. She's 'used up' anyway, but Shiatsu is MINE. She missed our last 'session' as I recall."

Shiatsu: "What the heck are you talking about? I never agreed to any 'last session' with you!"

Mercedes: "Oh, how cruel. You don't call, you don't write, and now you pretend you didn't know about our 'date' on your special night?"

Shiatsu: "You! You have NO right to demand my baby!"

Mercedes: "I have a right to demand anything I want! I'm the heir to the Oberhorns! The PRIZE is already mine, the Games are just a formality."

Shinobi: "Really? That's what Ash keeps saying. It can't be true though; only one guy gets the prize, so which one of you is lying?"

Clever move, Shinobi. Turn our opponents against each other, and while they're distracted, run away. Unfortunately, it doesn't work.

Ash: "HAHAHA! What a childish ploy. Did you think I would forget about you so easily? I'm willing to let Mercedes 'borrow' Shiatsu for a while. He gets bored with his 'toys' soon enough. But YOU won't get away! There's quite a bit of unfinished business between us, slave."

SHIT! We're really in trouble now. Ten to one odds put Alex in the hospital, unable to move for weeks, and his assailants were boys. We've got fifteen to one odds against us, and they might have powers. Even if the matriarch didn't set this up, she's certainly NOT going to stop it, and Martufe is only one man. He may not make it here in time to help us. Ash doesn't seem to care about going to exiled camp either, as long as he takes his pound of flesh, OUR flesh.

Just as we were cornered and about to lose hope, we hear Alex coming from the cafeteria. "Hey, what's taking so long? We're getting worried about you."

"Over here!" I cry out, but it really wasn't necessary. Alex can see our predicament, and with a simple clap, the others run to our aid. In terms of numbers, the odds are still against us. In terms of power though, it's anyone's guess how this will turn out.

Ash: "So the sissy came to rescue his whores, eh? Oh well, can't really blame him; after all, he doesn't have that many women to go around." His brides start laughing loudly at this, but a quick glance tells them to stop. It's obvious that this is a "canned" laugh, and was only done because Ash expects it, and refusal is not an option.

Alex: "Seems you have a terrible memory, Ash. I already told you they are not 'whores;' they are my BRIDES, but you won't catch me throwing the first punch."

Ash: "You dare view me as an equal, peasant!?"

Alex: "Of course, not. Perhaps there's someone out there who views you as an equal, but certainly not me. After all, it's hard to respect cowardice."

Ash: "Again you want to insult me! You are a bug I can crush at any time, maggot!"

Alex: "Oh? If you wanted to gauge my ladies' strength, you should have visited the training room after we left, or better still, interviewed the people training there now. We did go a bit overboard, but we were given permission first."

Ash: "So, being Martufe's 'pet' then?"

Alex: "No, I simply know good manners. Unlike some people I could mention."

Mercedes: "I see you're having trouble with Ash, here. Look, just give me back my Shiatsu, and I'll deal with him. In fact, just so I don't have too many girls, I'll even give you one of my other girls in return. What do you say?"

Alex's face grows dark with rage. "I said I would not strike the first blow, but I cannot possibly allow such an insult against my bride to pass. There is no way I would ever agree to such a thing, especially with someone who obviously treats his brides so poorly. Should you somehow manage to survive to the starting point, I will see you answer for it."

Mercedes: "She is MINE! I OWN HER!"

Alex: "She is not, and never has been your property. It is poor form for a man from such a 'pious' family as the Oberhorns to covet another man's wife. That IS a violation of the Ten Commandments, you know? What would your family say to the public if word gets out that their son spends his time living in sin?"

Alex: "Worse, what would happen when all those charities you visited, publicly learn that all those 'donations' you've made over the years have simply been done because you wore out your toys and didn't want them anymore, and that you, in fact, worship at the altar of Greed, one of the seven deadly sins? It would be best for you if you started acting like a MAN instead of a spoiled child wanting everything he sees."

Alex: "Let's go, ladies. We should enjoy our lunch before we completely lose our appetite."

Ash and Mercedes: "Come back here! We're not done with you!"

Alex: "Oh yes. Yes, you are. Anything else between us will be settled in the arena."

After we walk away, just out of sight, Alex begins shaking like a leaf with nervous exhaustion.

Sega: "That was so COOL!" (slaps Alex on the back.)

Atari: "Indeed. THAT is why we are here and will follow you anywhere, even to the depths of hell if need be."

Sierra: "Well said. We'll stand beside you whatever road you choose."

Shiatsu: "Perhaps it would have been better if I went with him."

Alex grabs me tightly. "Don't you dare! Don't leave me! He doesn't deserve you. **I** don't deserve you. Don't ever look down on yourself like that again! This goes for all of you. If you ever think of selling yourself off, even for my sake, I won't forgive you."

Diana: "Now THAT is how a MAN woos a lady!"

She suddenly hugs him. "And we're lucky to have you too. Don't ever sell yourself short either!"

It is quickly agreed after that close encounter that we are not to be out of each other's sight for any reason, at least not in the training center. Who knows what will happen in the arena. Alex's notes on the past Games show that there's only one constant in the arena: it is never the same way twice. We are already woefully outnumbered. We don't need to make it easy on them by dividing our strength.

After our lunch, we don't have any other plans for the day, and since there are no more available openings in the training grounds, we head back to our room to change out of our 'casual' clothes, bathe, and get into our pajamas. Certainly, we intended to simply enjoy each other's company while we could.

I'm still trying to get used to bathing with everyone. Alex and the others, however, simply are trying to make up for lost time, as it's an activity they all clearly missed dearly.

Even Shinobi was laughing and playing happily before everyone, though she never mentioned bathing with the others, only with Alex.

Sega: "What's up, little miss droopy?"

Shiatsu: "Huh? What? Oh, sorry, just... trying to get used to this."

Sega: "Have a lot on your mind, huh? I can tell." (splash as she sits down in the bathtub) "I don't blame you. It's a lot to take in."

Shiatsu: "How are you guys so comfortable being completely na-ked around him? Isn't it scary? Aren't you worried something might happen? How can you accept me so easily? Aren't you just a bit jeal-ous? You are all so open and honest, it's scary. I don't know how to cope with it at all!"

Diana: "Oh, we ARE jealous, dear, but we want him to be happy above everything else. We've known him all our lives, and he's al-ways been good to us. Of course, when we were little, it was easy to fool us with the whole 'she's just a special girl' thing his mom told us. Well, he IS special. While there aren't many men left in the world, we still know that 'those' are not normal for a boy, and like you said, they're real."

Shiatsu: "When did I say THAT?"

Sierra: "Sweetie, it's written all over your face. You're not the first 'street walker' to come before us. Shinobi was a real challenge. Scared, suspicious, maybe even a bit paranoid, she was as prickly as a porcupine. She was always trying to figure out what kind of 'lever-age' we wanted on her. Which reminds me, when we were growing up, each and every one of us was considerably stronger than Alex. If he HAD designs on us, we would have put him in his place, hard, and he knows it. He never even dreamed of trying to take us any-where we didn't want to go."

Why are Shinobi and Alex not chiming in? Well, they're in the sauna napping, with Shinobi on his chest. They didn't stay in the bath long, choosing just to get clean and then tend to Alex's wound in the sauna.

I know he didn't sleep well last night, though strangely, having him suck my breast in his sleep made me sleep more comfortably than I have in years. Even in the light of day, I still don't understand that. Shinobi couldn't have been sleeping well either, considering her crushing guilt on the night of Alex's capture. At least she's got the right approach going with Alex. She's got him relaxed; now she's just got to take the initiative and "boink" him silly without startling him.

Chapter Four

SIERRA: "STILL WITH us, sweetie?"

Shiatsu: "Ah! Yeah… I was just wondering if they were all right. I mean, they've been in that hot tub for a while."

Atari: "Oh… so you're wondering if she's going to make her move, eh?"

Shiatsu: "Wait, what? Where do you get that from?"

Diana: "Hehehe! Gotcha! You may think you're hiding things from us, but we can read you both like a book. We know she's had designs on him for a while. He just hasn't been ready. He may still not be ready, but we're not going to stand in the way. In fact, as his first, if you want to help them, we'll cheer you on, in our hearts. No way, we're going to cheer you out loud. That would be rude. It would also break the spell."

Sierra: "It was right of you to keep this away from Alex's ears though. We love him just the way he is, and his having an inflated ego would be a big turn off."

Shiatsu: "Since it's so normal for you to be… together with him, did you really break off the 'bath time' with him?"

They all sigh.

Diana: "No. WE didn't. Perhaps Alex doesn't know, but it's his mom who cut us off, though now I can see why. Ms. Dolorean is a real smart cookie. She knows how to read which way the wind blows. She must have seen this coming, and knew he'd need us."

Sierra: "Yes. If anything had happened, even if we started it, we would have been ineligible to become his brides. Even if we did something to put ourselves in debtor's prison like you, we would still have been ineligible. Got to hand it to that woman, she had her ear to the ground, that's for sure."

Shiatsu: "If she wanted you as maidens and him virginal, why buy Shinobi?"

Sega: "We all know his mother wants him happy as much as we do, if not more. He IS her life. Anything we say on this issue is pure speculation, as she didn't tell us what she was thinking. The most likely story is that she wanted a grandchild before she lost him. Unfortunately, that never came to be."

We suddenly hear a knock at the door.

Shiatsu: "I doubt it's the matriarch, but it could be a trap. You mind backing me up?"

Everyone nods in agreement.

Shiatsu: "Who is it!?"

"DELIVERY for Alex Dolorean!"

Shiatsu: "That's odd. BE THERE IN A MOMENT!"

Sierra: "I know it's a trap; you know it's a trap. If Alex were awake right now, he'd know it's a trap. Still, we can't act like we know it's a trap or they may do something drastic, like try to smoke us out."

The five of us grab our pajamas and dress quickly while heading to the door. I gently tap Alex and tell him, "Delivery. Get dressed." He groggily starts to move, then suddenly sees the look on my face and notices this is no ordinary event. He shakes Shinobi awake, gently but firmly, makes the sign for "silence," and they both get ready for battle also.

On a silent nod of agreement, I open the door carefully with the others watching my back, ready for anything, but what we see still takes us by surprise. It's not one of the other contestants. It's not the matriarch or her guard. It's not even members of other harems. It's the guards of the facility, bringing us what looks like dinner. "Martufe's orders. Tonight, everyone gets the evening meal delivered to their room. The facility is on lockdown. Nobody leaves their room unless instructed otherwise by Mr. Martufe over the intercom." A quick look down the hallway, with guards delivering packages to all the other rooms, helps to confirm the story. "Thank you. Any reason for this sudden change of status quo?"

Guard: "I have no information on that. You will have to inquire of him tomorrow. I can tell you that any unauthorized egress from your quarters will be severely and immediately punished. Please enjoy your meal; sleep well."

A quick salute, and she takes up guard position outside the door. One more quick look around and I close the door while bringing in the package. Whatever it is, it smells really good.

Shinobi: "Well, that's a first. Do you suppose this is in response to earlier?"

Alex: "Must be something unusual going on, like a 'sensitive' delivery of some kind for the arena. I am a bit wary of the meal though. It smells good, but is there any way to 'test' it?"

Immediate understanding comes to everyone. Alex suspects drugs or poison, and I can't blame him.

Atari: "It's not fool proof, but we have one way at our disposal." She cuts a small piece of the meal at random, and, before grasping the fork, summons a small flame, searing the fork.

Sega: "What are you doing?"

Atari: "Seeing if things burn in strange colors. It should rule out MOST drugs and poisons. Though, as I said, it's not fool proof."

She superheats the fork, and, seeing nothing burn or smoke, uses it to grab one piece of food at random from each dish burning them in turn. "I see nothing strange. Anyone else see anything?"

Alex: "I smell something sweet, a bit too sweet. Did you burn any candy, or a candied dish?"

Atari: "No…"

Shinobi's eyes widen. "Everyone, get down on the ground… NOW!"

We don't hesitate. Everyone gets on the ground in a hurry. Down the hall we hear cries of pain, agony, and death. Shinobi uses the sleeve of her pajama as a mask, and motions for us to do the same, and then directs us to the bathroom, namely the sauna. Copying what she does, we soak our sleeves and get back on the ground; after half an hour, the vents activate at full power. A noticeably female voice comes over the intercom. A voice we all recognize. "Congratulations on those of you who survived this surprise event. As some of you realized, the Games have begun! We're going to have a special 'surprise' each and every day. Look forward to it! HOHOHOHO! Today's 'prize' is the gourmet meal delivered to all the rooms. Enjoy the meal. It may be your last. Pleasant dreams!"

Shinobi: "How did you smell that? Aerosol nightshade poison is nearly impossible to detect by smell, at least before the concentration becomes lethal."

Alex: "I don't know! How would anyone else survive?"

Shinobi: "The odds are not good. If the food doesn't have the antidote, then either they were in some remote area of the room separated from the ventilation system, taking a shower so the water diluted the poison out of the air, or…"

Shiatsu: "What?"

Shinobi: "They survived because they were under the body of someone else who died instead."

Alex: "I still don't think the food is safe. If there's one 'surprise,' what's to prevent others?"

Shiatsu: "You can bet that the guards will 'punish' us with lethal force if we try to leave here."

We decide to put the "food" aside in a secure area, in case there are any more "surprises" in the packaging, and move to the bathroom to sleep there, in case of another gas attack. Even bringing the pillows, and as much of the padding as we can fit, it's still wildly uncomfortable, but beats being dead.

When all the others have finally wound down to sleep, I nudge Shinobi gently. "Now's your chance, kiddo." We know we're being watched, but at this point, we just don't care anymore. I let her know that she had the right idea with the sauna earlier, but that the "surprise" ruined her moment. After years of trying to coax him out of his shell, without success, she doesn't have any confidence in going after him alone. We agree that it's best to go after him together. What we didn't know was that the others were only pretending to sleep. They knew what was going on, and gave each other the "thumbs-up" sign all the way. Once we get him out of his shell, and engage him in a *ménage a trois*, not only do I get a second helping of his loving, but Shinobi also gets to see how good he is herself. In fact, she's so happy; she's crying tears of joy.

Unfortunately, it doesn't last. When we SHOULD be enjoying the afterglow, Alex suddenly cries out, "NO! Don't leave me! Please, don't let them take her away!"

This shocks everyone in the room. All pretenses the others were making about sleeping are instantly abandoned. So it's not sex that he's afraid of. Sex is just a trigger for something else, some deep-seated terror that shakes him to the core. He is so terrified, he doesn't even hear us. We all have to hold him and rock him gently until he finally calms down, reminding him over and over that we're not going to leave him.

Once he finally goes to sleep, Shinobi looks accusingly at me and goes, "What was that? You NEVER mentioned anything like this."

Shiatsu: "Remember, we didn't get an afterglow during my time with him. We were... interrupted immediately. He was terrified, but there was an armed invasion going on. There was nothing like this."

Sierra: "It's not her fault, dear. It's not your fault either. There was absolutely no way to know something like that would have happened."

Atari: "What…what have they done to him? Nothing I know about our machines could explain that."

Diana: "That had to be the result of some serious psychological trauma, a serious 'abandonment' issue. What though? He's an only child, his mother never abandoned him, and none of us in this room did either."

Sega: "He didn't have any other friends, boy or girl that we know of. We are definitely missing something. Some piece of the puzzle is missing. You shouldn't get up; just stay with him all night, so he doesn't have another 'episode.' Don't worry; we'll take care of you."

Indeed they do. They make sure to cover our nakedness, pulling up the covers and tucking us in. I know it's not my fault, but it still makes me weep. Seeing the guy who has treated me so well, someone willing to go up against incredible odds, even challenging the matriarch for my sake, suffer hurts me deeply.

I know that bitch is watching and sadistically laughing with evil glee at our heartache. We suspect that the encounter was broadcast to the audience at large, just like the 'surprise event' with the gas, but we don't know how the audience at large is reacting right now. We even know it was being run on the internal security network, and that the guards are betting on whether we'll even make it to the arena, and even Martufe can't stop them as it's an officially sanctioned activity.

What we don't know is that Alex's mother is also being forced to watch in her cell, purely for the sake of making her suffer. Weeping with regret, she cries out, "My baby! I'm sorry, so, so sorry. It's all my fault! I've hurt you so much, my sweet, innocent, little boy!"

The guards outside her cell cruelly record her grief-ridden words, smirking as she cries herself to sleep.

Meanwhile…. at Martufe's office:

Martufe: "Are you certain about this?!"

Guard: "Yes, sir. We ran the DNA comparison check the maximum one hundred times to be sure."

Martufe: "This explains so much. So that Dolorean woman found a way, eh? What a clever girl. But wait, this test shows a fifty percent match to me for two people, and a rather large matching percentage between them. I thought he had no siblings."

Guard: "Yes, that IS what the records show, sir. We truly have no family record on the bride."

Martufe: "So somebody's been 'naughty.' Poor kids, and now here they are fighting for their lives. So it seems the 'if we can't control it, we'll destroy it' mentality is in play, doesn't it?"

Guard: "I… wouldn't know, sir."

Martufe: "Of course, not. Dismissed, and I shouldn't have to tell you not to mention this to ANYONE, especially not the matriarch, right?"

Guard: "Understood. SIR!"

After the guard leaves, Martufe sighs and proclaims, "There must be something I can do to help them; they are my heirs after all! Fate is such a cruel and fickle mistress with a very wicked sense of humor, isn't she?"

The following morning, I awaken to find the four elementals watching us with a very mischievous look on their faces. It isn't long before I notice why.

Diana: "So 'that' is catching, eh? Don't worry, Shiatsu, you're not alone this time."

Sure enough, Shinobi is doing "that" too. Looks like Alex was getting his breasts sucked in stereo while sleeping. He looks very comfortable though. Guess the nightmares are over, for now.

Sierra: "Oh, don't worry. We put a bit of effort into it and memorialized this moment for you."

Shiatsu: "Eh? What? I thought we didn't have the equipment to take pictures."

Sega: "Oh, no. We did something better."

She proceeds to pull out a ceramic plate, showing a scene of Alex, Shinobi, and I sleeping peacefully with Shinobi and me suckling as Alex holds us tight. Embarrassing as it is, I have to admit it's well made.

Shiatsu: "You used your powers to make that?"

Atari: "Indeed. We've got to treasure these precious moments while we can. We might not get another chance."

A scratching sound on the bathroom door gets us out of our reverie. We move to investigate and find… evidence of large animals having been in the bedroom. Seems like some are still here, dead. They found our "dinner." Alex was right. It was poisoned.

Shinobi: "They all show signs of nightshade poisoning. So it wasn't a gas attack. The smell was only from the piece you burned, Atari. Either they set off the vents as a distraction or the smoke was just enough to trip the sensors. Considering the matriarch, I think it's the former."

Shiatsu: "So sleeping in the bathing room was the right decision after all."

Alex: "What happened? Has everyone been crying?"

So he doesn't remember the outburst, or what he said that night about having his sister taken away? Good, saves some rather difficult discussions for a later time. At least now we know how fragile he truly is.

Alex: "Eh? What? Why are my friends here?" (looks closer) "Wait! These aren't my friends. They don't have the right number of claws, and they have fans at their neck... POISON SPITTERS! My friends told me about them."

Is Alex saying he can communicate with dinosaurs now?

Shiatsu: "Your friends? You can speak with raptors and wolves?"

Sierra: "Doesn't surprise me. He's always been good with animals."

Shinobi: "Now this is new. I think we need to hear this."

Sega: "Oh, yeah. Alex found a kitten once. Lost, scared, obviously abused. After nursing the cat back to health, he tracked down the brat who tortured it, and demanded an apology. Brat tried pushing Alex around. Alex beat the ever-loving snot out of her. Brat never went near kittens again."

Diana: "Yeah, the phrase 'a little birdie told me' has been literally true for Alex on numerous occasions."

Alex: "I don't do well with poison animals. I don't think they're gone, too much 'food' here."

Of course, he means US!

Alex: "We need goggles, something to protect our eyes. If the poison gets in your eyes, it wil l paralyze you, making you an easy kill."

While searching the room for anything we could use, Alex stumbles upon the plate the girls made. "Beautiful. Absolutely gorgeous and very well, made. THANK YOU!" The tears of joy in his eyes are more than enough reward for them. He then stumbles on the shards of glass from the broken window/door where the animals came in. "Can you do something with these?"

Atari: "Hmm, clever. We don't need to correct vision; we just need to protect our eyes, right? Quickly, everyone, gather up the glass shards; we'll need to find something to use as a frame, but these shards could easily be crafted into lenses."

Sega goes into the bathroom and brings back the rings from the shower curtain.

Sega: "What about these to hold the glass?"

Atari: "Hmm, not bad, but we need two more. We've got fourteen eyes, and there's twelve here, unless someone wants to go without."

Diana: "The napkin holders from our 'gourmet meal,'...will they work?"

Atari: "Hmm, the size is a bit different from the shower curtain rings, but we should have more than enough glass to fill them. All that's missing now is some string, wire, cloth, and something that can hold the frames together and keep them on our heads."

Everyone: "All right!"

While we're preparing, screams of terror, desperation, and death continue throughout the halls. These are soon followed by the sound of gunfire. Gunfire? What could that mean? I doubt it's the guards chasing away the Diplodysius, aka, "poison spitters." away. Most likely it's a "clean-up" crew going after anyone who's not dead or dying. We need to hurry and be battle ready, because the sounds are growing closer.

Atari: "All right, the laces from our 'formal' shoes will have to do. Everyone, cover me while I work on these. I won't be able to defend myself and craft these glasses at the same time."

We quickly take up defensive formations around Atari while she gets to work. I only hope she's ready before whatever's shooting gets here. We don't have the time to ponder that, as the poisonous dinosaurs return to the broken door, hissing. Alex throws the rest of the "dinner" that was prepared for us at them, and when they turn their backs on us to chase after it, we let them have it. Doubting we'll be so lucky next time, we take the beds apart and erect a barricade over the broken door, using the bed frames as slats. We know it won't hold long, but it's the best we can do.

Atari: "Finished! Everyone, grab a pair. Don't bother changing into 'our casual clothes.' We don't have the time."

She's right. We briefly consider going outside, but decide against it. There's no telling how many of those dinosaurs are out there, or if there's something, bigger, meaner, and nastier herding them towards us. We have to take a gamble and head into the corridor. Good thing too, because the pounding on our barricade begins in earnest, and we doubt we'll be able to fight off the waves of enemies that lie behind the siege.

In the hallway, there are no guards. That immediately is a bad sign. Another bad sign is that many of the harem suite room doors stand ajar with no sound coming from them.

A quick examination of these rooms shows that those who didn't die from their "last meal" were killed and eaten. A search also reveals nothing that can be used in a valid tactical manner. Seems when

Martufe said the rooms were searched and emptied, he meant it.

We decide to head towards the training room. Not only is it fortified, but also there are the training outfits, which are better clothes for fighting than our pajamas, and there are weapons, even if they are made of wood and fragile. We know others may have had the same idea, but it's the best option at the moment.

We turn the corner and run right into the source of the gunfire we heard earlier:, roving tank tread robots with machine gun turrets. As I suspected, they were not sent with the purpose of clearing out the dinosaurs; they were sent to target us! The confirmation is the dot from the laser sight on our chests, and the loading of ammunition.

Alex: "Take cover!"

Alex summons and throws a shuriken at the lead robot, disabling its camera. Without hesitation, we all dive into the open suite doors. Moments later, a barrage of bullets rains down on where we just were.

Alex: "Ouch! Everyone OK?!"

Everyone: "We're all accounted for."

When the robots start firing into the rooms, we take cover behind anything we can, beds, walls next to the doors, anything. Our counter attacks don't seem to do anything. Even the elemental powers just bounce off. I can't get close enough to use my blades, and the shuriken Alex used only broke a camera; the rest of the robotic body is just too heavily armored. It's true that they can't move quickly, but they don't have to in these narrow corridors; and even if we could close the doors, they can concentrate their fire and blast right through them.

Alex: "Sierra, Diana, Atari, Sega. Combine your powers. It's our only hope!"

The training we did yesterday pays off in spades. We are all able to read and time our moves perfectly. Sierra and Diana summon a sandstorm that clogs the robot's joints, reducing their mobility to the point of almost making them statues. Atari and Sega create a cloud of steam, reducing their visibility to nil, and allowing Shinobi and me to get close with blades and cut them to pieces. The next wave of robots gets a different elemental mix. Atari and Diana summon an inferno so hot it melts their outer housing and fries their wiring.

The wave after that, Sega and Sierra call upon a mud slide that crushes the water-proof casing, rendering it useless in protecting the electronic gear within. In very short order, we eliminate all the robot drones sent against us.

We take the machine guns and all the ammunition we can carry. Atari takes some of the electronic gear inside the robots, saying only "It might be useful later." We shrug and make backpacks out of the victims' clothes to make all this stuff easier to carry, and resume heading towards the combat training room.

The matriarch "supervisor" who was watching, and is running the Games, was beside herself with rage. "What was R&D doing?! Those robots were supposed to be unstoppable, yet that brat, Alex Dolorean, with his handful of whores took them apart like TOYS! Worse, they're now armed with heavy assault weapons, giving them a clear advantage over everyone else! Were those idiots at R&D spending those millions we gave them on porn and online video games? Control! Use the collars; send every beast we've got in there at Alex Dolorean. I don't care how you do it, TAKE HIM OUT!" She then smashes her cell phone against the wall. "Incompetent bunglers!"

Although we could not hear it, the audience at large was cheering us on. Odds makers were listing us as "THE team to beat," and both Ms. Dolorean and Martufe were quite proud of us.

When we reach the training room, our hearts sink into our stomachs. The place is a total loss. Dead contestants lay everywhere, the weapons are gone or destroyed, and the doors are smashed to kindling.

While we're contemplating what to do next, we hear the shrieking sound of a large reptile heading our way. "SKRRIIEEEE!!"

Alex: "We've got to move! Anyone got some ideas?"

Sierra: "We could try the cafeteria."

Alex: "No good. Sure, there's food, water, and plenty of cover, but there's too many entrances and exits. We'd be overwhelmed in a hurry."

Shiatsu: "What about the 'bride selection' area? I can't speak for food, but there are water fountains, only one entrance and exit, and even cages where we were 'displayed' for the choosing ceremony."

Alex: "Perfect. Shiatsu, please lead the way. You were the only one of us there."

Shiatsu: "Gladly. Let's go before our dinosaur 'friends' find us."

We first backtrack to our room, what's left of it, and then go to the infirmary where Alex was treated, and finally head for the bridal selection room with the dreaded shrieking going on all the while. When we arrive, we immediately take up positions for maximum crossfire effectiveness and hunker down for a siege. We don't have to wait long. As expected, the "poison spitters" start to swarm through the entrance. We open fire, but their persistence is unnerving. One of them goes down, and the one behind him climbs over his body to get at us, or try anyway. We barely have time to reload before the next wave comes. This isn't normal predator behavior. Normally when predators face overwhelming resistance, they move on to easier prey, unless driven mad with hunger. In this case, hunger doesn't seem the cause. It's like they're being controlled.

Atari: "I knew it! Shock collars. They're being controlled remotely and 'sent' here."

Everyone: "Eh!?"

Atari: "Focus on the battle for now. I'll explain during the next lull!"

When the next lull does come, and we get a chance to catch our breaths, Atari states, "Look closely at their bodies. What do you see?" Sure enough, there's some kind of mechanical device connected to their necks.

Sierra: "Those things were designed for ranchers to keep their herds from straying off, also to make sheep shearing and slaughter for meat easier. Now they're being used for this? I almost feel sorry for these animals, they're not really animals anymore; they are puppets. Those collars over-ride the brain and cause the animal's body to do what the controller wants instead."

Atari: "I figured they'd do something like this. I mean, if there was no control, why let the animals loose in the facility? Without control collars, it would be damn hard to get them all out again."

Shinobi: "By the way, seems my little 'theory' yesterday was correct. Did you notice the weapon Alex used in the battle with the robots?"

She's right. Alex summoned and used a shiruken, also known as a throwing or ninja star. Previously, Alex could only summon blades. He has seemingly copied Shinobi's primary ability.

Atari: "That...—that's good to know, but now isn't the best time to discuss it. Anyway, the reason I got those robot parts is that we can build something to jam/disable the collars, but we'll probably only get to use it once."

Alex: "If you can build it, do so. We'll cover you."

Atari: "Are you sure?"

Alex: "Positive. If they've 'collared' my friends, I don't want to be forced to kill them." His face takes on a rare, grim determination.

Atari: "All right. I can't guarantee it will work, but I'll build it for you."

Alex: "Thanks!" He then pets Atari's head in gratitude.

Atari: (blushing furiously) "D...don't do that while I work!"

The rest all start smirking and snickering at each other as if they're saying, "Guess who's going to be next."

A howl coming down the corridor confirms Alex's fear. Dire wolves are coming for us.

Alex: "SHE has to be behind this. There's no other explanation. "

Everyone nods in full understanding.

Alex: "OK, everyone. Hold your fire until the last possible moment. I don't want to hurt them more than absolutely necessary. We are going to need them, in the arena."

Chapter Five

IT WAS EXACTLY as Alex figured; the collars on the wolves are obvious, but the wolves are not alone. A pack of Velociraptors are there also. Rather than rushing in blindly like the others, they stop and glare at us, growling and snarling, as if they're waiting for something.

Alex: "Skae lee? Mai Fang?"

I still find it ridiculous that he calls a raptor "scaly" and a dire wolf "my fang," but whatever works, works. The look of recognition on their faces is clearly palpable. They are definitely Alex's pets or "friends" as he calls them. Perhaps they're not waiting, but are actively resisting the collars. In any event, none of us let our guard down. They could attack at any moment, and we know it. They must know it too. In moments, I see signs of distress from them.

While I don't understand the howls, growls, shrieks, and cries coming from them explicitly, Alex seems to know them quite well.

<Help us!> <It hurts!> <Furless cub, we are being forced to attack. It hurts to refuse!>

<Warm blood! FREE US!>

Alex surprisingly responds in kind. <We are trying. The machines on your neck, they must be stopped first, or you will die.>

<We prefer death over harming our Alpha!>

<Free us from the pain!>

<Quickly! Or we attack!>

Alex: "They're going to attack soon. They can't hold out much longer!"

Atari: "Damn circuit boards refuse to cooperate. Give me just a few more minutes!"

Unfortunately, we don't have the time. One of the raptors leaps at us, and Alex guns it down before it literally bites my head off. It isn't long before the others start attacking in earnest, although some have collapsed purely from the effort of resistance.

Being faster, more agile, and stronger than the "poison spitters" we fought earlier, and since the one controlling them has learned from the moves we used, as well as the fact that we don't want to kill the wolves and raptors has made our battle far more difficult. Avoiding injuries is no longer possible. We all do our best to keep the injuries out of vital locations, and the animals away from Atari.

Atari: "At last! Finished!" She primes and activates the device.

Atari must be a brilliant engineer. The device works like a charm. All the animals stop attacking us immediately.

Alex: <Quickly! Go after the machines on your necks!>

Sega: "Everyone, gather your powers and target those collars!"

Even on the streets, I've never seen a fur ball like this! Sheer mayhem ensues as the animals try to rip the collars off each other; the elementals try to soak, bury, blow apart, or fry them, and Alex and Shinobi try to take them out with precise shots from summoned projectiles. I feel totally useless because if I try running in there with my blade, I will just get torn apart, and machine guns are not designed for precise shots. All I can do now is hang back and watch in case the collars reactivate. Fortunately, they do not. All that remains of them is twisted metal and pieces of scrap.

Atari: "I knew it. We won't be able to use THIS again." She holds forward the device she worked on so hard. It's a smoking ruin.

Alex: "You did well, Atari. You saved us, all of us." This time, Atari lets him pat her head, happily.

Indeed, although many of the animals are badly wounded, and we've got some injuries ourselves, none of us died. I begin to move amongst us to treat our injuries, using my limited field experience from the nurse's office where I worked before being sent here, and from my time on the streets. When I get to the animals though, they view me with hostility and suspicion.

Alex: <Stop. Do not harm her. She will help you.> "Go ahead, treat them, Shiatsu."

While they still look at me with suspicion and hostility, the animals make no move to attack, nor do they offer resistance. When they notice that I'm treating their wounds, the hostility disappears, but the suspicion does not. As soon as I complete treating them, Alex again speaks to them.

Alex: <Grab the "poison spitters" you can carry and leave here quickly. The "bad people" will be here soon, and we won't be able to stop them.>

<We want to fight!> <We will protect you!> <We will make enemy, bleed, hurt, die!>

Alex: <No! Enemy is strong. Go. Hide. Watch. Wait for weakness!>

The animals look at each other and, after showing submission before Alex, run out of sight, perhaps leaving the facility. They, of course, take some of the corpses with them, probably for food.

Alex: "That's probably not the end of today's 'surprise,' but that's all we can do for now."

Matriarch: "What happened? Why didn't the raptors and wolves rip them to shreds?!"

Control: "Some sort of high- energy pulse overwhelmed the collars' RF input. While we were trying to compensate, the collars were removed and/ or destroyed. The animals then fled the facility."

Matriarch: "DAMN IT! Where did you people get this equipment? Did the label say 'made in China' at some point?"

(Cultural note: Prior to the fall of China, numerous international safety advisories about substandard, defective, and/ or dangerous merchandise, and China's penchant for slave labor took a heavy toll on the reputation of their goods. So much so that "made in China" became synonymous with "junk." Even after the fall, the label stuck.)

Control: "Sorry, Madame Matriarch. I am not in a position to answer that inquiry. Perhaps you should speak to someone at requisitions?"

Matriarch: "Don't get 'cute' with me! Arrgh! Guess I have to call an end to today's 'surprise.' End transmission." The video conference between the matriarch and "control" ends. "Your luck will run out soon, Alex Dolorean. Just you wait. When I'm done with you, you'll wish those pets of yours had ripped you to pieces."

She sends a transmission over the intercom. "Attention, contestants. Congratulations. Today's 'surprise' is at an end. All survivors please come to the cafeteria for a bit of rest, relaxation, and your mid-day meal while the maintenance bots repair, renovate, and clean up the facilities."

We look at each other carefully. Tired, injured, and running low on ammunition, we figure that even though this is most likely a trap, we had better go. The "maintenance bots" will most likely be more heavily armed than we are. Since we skipped last night's "dinner" and we had no breakfast, we need food as well. Keeping our weapons fully loaded, we move out.

Surprisingly, we arrive at the cafeteria without further incident. It's no surprise that the place is far emptier than when we were here yesterday. What IS surprising is the number of survivors. Ash Udderweis and his ten lackeys, with all their harems, are here with no more injuries than when the Games started. (That is VERY suspicious.)

Mercedes Oberhorn is here, but he has lost a good third of his harem, probably sacrificed them to beasts so he could get away. If that's his "strategy," then I'm glad I DID NOT go with him.

Arcades Allbright, his thrall Kakizaki Ikari, and Tendo Akaneda stand out, and seem pretty intact. (Alex made VERY detailed notes about the most "dangerous" opponents we would be likely to face, so it's hard not to recognize them.) Everyone turns and notices us, battered, bruised, but alive, and armed to the teeth. Much as we would like to be left alone to enjoy our meal, we are obviously NOT ignored. Well, I can't really blame them. Most of them are only alive because they managed to hide or went unnoticed while the animals and attack bots went after someone else, most likely us.

In short, somewhere around 50 percent of the contestants have been "eliminated." Most, if not all, of the remaining "neutral" players immediately gathered around us and began peppering us with questions. Alex was polite, cordial, and friendly, but he didn't say anything that would have revealed our strengths, weaknesses, or tactics.

"Where did you get the guns?"

Alex: "We took them from the wreckage of assault bots that attacked us."

"No way, you guys took down the security bots?"

Alex: "With great difficulty, yes."

"How did you get past the animals that got in?"

Alex: "We shot them, and some ran away."

"Where did you hole up? How did you take down the bots?"

Alex: "That's a SECRET! If you survive, you'll get to see the footage."

This goes on for a while until the food is brought out. The chef herself explicitly comes to us and says, "I promise, there's no poison in this meal." To prove it, she samples a piece of every dish in front of everyone. "I truly hope you enjoy it. My pride as a chef is counting on it. It's been so long since I had real ingredients."

When Alex sees the platter, he calmly, quietly, but forcefully proclaims, "Excuse us, please. There is something we have to do."

Alex, and all the others bow their heads and fold their hands, as if in prayer.

Shinobi: "I know you're new and don't know the custom, but please, do as we do, as best you can. It's an important tradition in our families when receiving a true meal, especially with meat."

Alex: "Dear Lord, our father in heaven, thank you for those that who died so that we may live. Thank you for providing the animals of the field and allowing us to partake of their meat. Thank your Son for giving his life to save our souls. Thank you for bringing us all together to enjoy your company and many blessings, and for our health and well being. In HIS holy name, Amen."

Everyone: "AMEN!"

Why does this prayer sound so familiar? I'm sure I never heard it before, but something about it reminds me of home, family, and the love of my mother. But I clearly remember my mother cruelly throwing me out onto the streets to fend for myself, with not even a coin of my own. Suddenly I begin weeping with conflicting emotions.

Alex: "Shiatsu? What's wrong? You're crying."

Shiatsu: "I...I don't know. I swear I've never heard that prayer before, yet it sounds so familiar. It reminds me of 'home,.' some place I'll never see again."

Alex: "It's all right. I will never abandon you, no matter what happens."

Everyone: "WE won't abandon you either. Come, let us not dishonor the animals whose meat was prepared for us, and eat."

I dry my tears, and try for a meager smile. "Yeah. Let's eat."

Suddenly all the "neutrals" who were gathered around us scatter. "He's one of 'them!' He's a Christo-PAGAN! Stay back or his witches will curse you!"

"They drink blood in their wine!"

"They eat human flesh baked into their bread!"

"They worship a naked MAN hanging on a tree! Stay away! STAY AWAY!"

"They have the power to control DEMONS! Stay as far away as you can!"

Even Ash Udderweis momentarily loses his "I'm superior to you" façade and cowers in terror.

The only one unphased is Tendo Akaneda, who seems to be praying over his meal with his harem also, but instead of saying anything aloud simply makes a "t" sign in the air.

Alex whispers to me, "Don't be afraid. Everything those poor fools are saying is either a deliberate mis-interpretation of the Holy Gospel by which we live, or an outright lie. There is no truth in any of the propaganda they've obviously been fed. Enjoy your meal. We're going to need our strength tomorrow."

I nod and eat my meal quietly. Although I know Alex believes what he's telling me is true, I've only heard bad things about the "Christo-pagan" faith. I've also seen the Matriarchy send troops to crack down heavily on places where "The Christ" was worshipped. They usually don't mobilize the Matriarch Elite Troops on anything short of armed rebellion, but they always mobilize on rumor of a "Christio-pagan" church.

We didn't notice at the time, but when the cook heard Alex's prayer, she brought a cross-shaped object from her pocket, kissed it, and mouthed the words, "Thank you, Lord." Alex, did notice, and merely nodded at her with an approving look before she hid her cross again and returned to the kitchen.

After we finished our meal, Alex instructed us to return to our room, provided we were allowed entry, where he intended to explain everything to me. Our room's damage was very minor, so it was repaired quickly, and we were granted entry. Once inside, I thought we would go to the bath, especially the sauna since Sega noted that there were various healing ingredients in the water, but Alex shook his head and bade we sit down, for there was much to discuss.

Alex: "Shiatsu, I know this is all very sudden for you, and you have many doubts and fears. Yes, I am a 'Christo-pagan,' and so are the others. Shinobi converted when my mother bought her servitude."

Shinobi: "Yes. It was very easy for me to believe there's a 'supreme God' watching over me when I found myself in the Dolorean home where I am welcomed, and loved, as opposed to the fate I truly deserved, death or worse, enslavement to someone like Ash Udderweis."

Shiatsu: "You said that what the others said in the cafeteria was, at best, a deliberate misinterpretation. Can we start there?"

Alex: "Certainly. The whole 'drink blood in the wine, and human flesh in the bread' statement is a bastardization of Holy Communion, where we use wine and bread as a symbol for the time an innocent man went to death in a murderer's place, and, in doing so, saved us all from eternal damnation, if only we believed in him and followed his teachings. As for the 'authority over demons,' while that is LITERALLY true, the intention implied is not. We don't summon demons, and we certainly don't command them to do harm to others."

Alex: "Supposedly, we have authority to cast them out, both from the body and from where people live, though none have been qualified to do the ritual for centuries. In fact, all but the most basic knowledge of it is lost. The primary reason for this is, if you're not aware, simply possessing a written copy of the Holy Scripture is punishable by death, by will of the Matriarchy. When things are passed on orally, mistakes tend to happen, more often than when passed on in written form at least. As for the 'witches' thing, regrettably, there was a dark time when our ancestors hunted other faiths as witches and burned them alive. Christo-pagans don't have witches."

Shiatsu: "Where did this religion come from?"

Alex: "Surprisingly, Israel, one of the few countries that existed from 'Before Man' (B.M.) and still does. In fact, we consider the Jewish holy book, the Torah, the first half of our Holy Scripture. It is actually legal even here, but the only copies we can get are in either Aramaic or Hebrew. "

Alex: "Attempting to smuggle a copy in our language has severe penalties, including Exile Island, and death. As far as I am aware, Israel is the only country in the world that is NOT in the Matriarchy, and does not participate in the Games. Immigration there is very tight, technology we take for granted here does not exist, and to this day, the country is surrounded by enemies desiring its destruction and the death of all its citizens. Life is very harsh and dangerous there, but they produce the vast majority of the world's food, and their people are VERY skilled warriors with the most powerful weapons ever known to man. The Jewish religion won't be disappearing any time soon."

Shiatsu: "Does your faith allow for slaves?" I look at Shinobi.

Alex: "Yes, with very narrow restrictions. Further, slave owners are admonished to treat slaves as employees, meaning a fair wage, as family, or both. Shinobi is family, and she knows it, especially now that she is my bride. Don't misunderstand. We don't CONDONE slavery. If we could, we'd smash the institution. We've done it before. Unfortunately, we've got our hands full just trying to survive."

Shiatsu: "Does it allow for polygamy, or harems?"

Alex: "Absolutely. The founder of Israel had two wives, twelve sons, and at least one daughter, Dinah. When the prince of a country raped her and tried to make her his wife after the fact, her twelve brothers went and killed him, the king, and all the royal army. Our faith does NOT look well upon rape and violation. Unfortunately, going purely by the evidence at hand, I cannot truthfully say the same about 'the Faith of the Goddess.'"

Everyone nods at that statement.

Alex: "The founder of Israel wasn't alone. Various Jewish kings had multiple wives, the most famous of which were David, with at least a dozen, and Solomon, the Wise, with twice that many. The Torah states that all those women were VERY happy. Well, all except David's first wife. After David saved her life from her own father, who wanted to make her a sacrifice unto a pagan god, and married her, she caught him dancing before God, and got jealous. Long story short, she basically went to David and said, 'It's me or God!' He, of course, said, 'God,' locked her up in a tower, and she died a childless virgin, which was a terrible curse back then."

Atari: "That's why we keep a tight lid on our jealousy, dear."

Sega: "Indeed. As long as you try to make Alex happy (Note: making

Alex happy means treating us well too), we have no objections. But if you're only trying to take advantage of him, or are actively trying to hurt him, the fangs and claws will come out."

Alex: "Polygamy fell out of favor with our faith a while back because it was abused. It came back into fashion after the outbreak when it became obvious that there just weren't enough men around to keep monogamy viable."

We spend the next few hours going over the history of Alex's faith, which includes how it became illegal, starting with lawsuits from various self-proclaimed atheist groups to Barack Hussein Obama's dedicated persecution of Christianity, where various executive orders, rules, regulations, and the wildly unpopular (over 70 percent of the American population opposed it) Obama health care law forced Christian institutions to not only openly embrace abortion, which all devout Christians consider murder, but also imposed stiff penalties both civil and criminal if Christian hospitals and clinics refused to perform them. (There were quite a few politicians who went to church one or two hours a week, but spent the rest of the week bathing themselves in innocent blood, in the eyes of believers, for money and power.) Catholic institutions were forced by executive order not only to distribute contraception, in clear violation of their faith, but also to do so for free; marry homosexuals in same-sex unions, again in clear violation of religious doctrine; and withstand obvious prejudice against them in disputes with other faiths. It all finally culminated during the peak of the outbreak where God took the blame, and the 'Faith of the Goddess' came into being. Alex also points out several "accepted pagan" rituals that he knows were assimilated into the faith for the sake of camouflage, but became official.

Shinobi: "Basically, it's the same as going around poking a

Peacekeeper in the eye at every opportunity, and then getting angry when something happens, and she's not able to protect you."

Alex: "Well put. To be technically accurate, while we're often accused of being a 'crazy cult,' the definition of cult fits 'the Faith of the Goddess' far better. There have been no verifiable 'miracles' that can be directly attributed to this 'Goddess, who came to avenge the injustice inflicted upon women for centuries,' unless you want to consider the outbreak a 'miracle.' There ARE, however, verifiable miracles backing up our faith. The most notable of these is the death and resurrection of our savior. The grave, which still exists, not only has been verified as having been opened from the inside after our savior was buried, but the interior was also exposed to extreme light, the brightness having only been matched by the light of a nuclear explosion. Of course, there was no nuclear explosion back then, not only because nuclear weapons didn't exist, but also because Israel would be a smoking, radioactive pit if there was."

Shinobi: "I know it's a big decision, and you won't be forced to join us, but it would be a big help if you were a fellow believer."

Alex: "I'm flattered, Shinobi, but even as the senior member here, I'm still not qualified to baptize her."

Sega: "As 'oracle of water,' I am, Alex."

Shiatsu: "I... I don't know. I WANT to believe you all, I really do. You've been nothing but kind to me. If you were a bad person, Alex, you would have taken Mercedes's offer without hesitation."

Shiatsu: "But still, I've heard so many bad things..."

Alex hugs me tight to his bosom and pats my head gently. "It's all right, Shiatsu. This is your immortal soul we're talking about, as well as the fact that ours is a VERY persecuted faith. I wasn't expecting an immediate decision, but I am glad you came to us and asked."

Everyone: "As are we. You are always welcome."

Shiatsu: "Thanks, everyone." (sniff) "I don't know about the rest of you, but these clothes and my body have seen better days. I think it would be a good idea to wash up.?"

Alex: "Yeah. Our clothes do need some work, and we've got quite a few injuries that need mending. Unless anyone wants to go get some dinner, I say we call it a day. No telling what 'surprise' is in store for us tomorrow."

Sierra: "Let's get dinner and then call it a day. We don't know when we'll get to eat again."

Diana: "Well, that's certainly true. We should at least change though before our clothes fall off."

Sega: "Agreed, and then when we return, we'll clean up. If only I had a needle and thread, I could fix these, easily."

This time, we are left alone in the cafeteria, except for the head chef who touches her forehead, then her lips, then her sternum. Alex returns the gesture, and we sit to eat. Since there is no meat, only fresh fruits and vegetables, the prayer is not said.

Shiatsu: "What was that gesture with the cook?"

Alex: "Seems we found someone we can trust."

Shiatsu: "So that's why..."

Diana touches my lips with her index finger. "Dearie, remember, we are being watched and heard here." I nod quietly. We eat our meal in peace, and return to our room. We hang our jerkins in a place where they can be grabbed and put on quickly; our pajamas indeed don't look like they will survive being worn again, and we all rinse in the bathtub, and then proceed to squeeze into the sauna. "Ouch, that stings." is a common outcry.

After a few minutes of relaxation, Atari suddenly decides to straddle Alex. "D-...don't misunderstand! This-...this is just because there's not enough room to sit normally!"

Sega: "Right."

Diana: "Mmm-hmm! Sure."

Sierra: "Of course, whatever you say."

Their voices are full of mischievous sarcasm. Meanwhile Shinobi puts her hands to her face but is peeking through her fingers, and I just don't know where to look.

Alex begins kissing Atari, starting at the belly and working his way up...

Atari: "Hey! What do you think you're doing?"

Alex: "Don't misunderstand. I'm just kissing your wounds to make them better."

Atari: (blushing) "Oh. That's OK, then."

Everyone: "Oooh!"

Alex then gently runs his index fingers up her sides, starting at the hips and ending at the armpits. It's easy to see that she REALLY enjoys that. It isn't long before the pretenses fall away, and they begin "getting naughty" in earnest.

Diana: "You can do THAT with your tongue?"

Sega: "You can put that THERE?"

Sierra: "Oh. Oh! MY!"

Shinobi: "This is so embarrassing." Seeing the red flare out on her ears, she must be blushing furiously.

We are all getting splashed with the sauna water as Atari bounces up and down.

Atari: "Hey! You in the peanut gallery! Could you maybe stop with the play-by-play? It's distracting, and we're distracted enough already!"

Alex: "Um. Where were we?"

Atari : "See!?"

Everyone: (embarrassed) "Sorry."

Atari: "We were doing … this." And she begins sucking on Alex's breasts while tracing the armpits with her fingers.

Alex: "Ooh! Yeah! Just like that!"

Atari's eyes narrow as she realizes she was tricked, and she glares at Alex. "Hey!"

Alex reaches up and cups her face. "Well, at least we're not 'distracted' any more, right?"

Everyone: "Ooh! How sly!"

This really gets her motor running, and she quickly gets pushed over the edge. She bends back like a bow in the final moments and cries out, "HNGG! YES! OH! YES!"

This in turn brings Alex to the finish line! As soon as they sigh, completely satisfied, everyone suddenly claps and cheers, loudly. Alex and Atari blush so hard, their faces match her hair.

Shiatsu: "Is this part of your faith? I mean, this isn't the first time I've been in the audience. In fact, I've even been 'on stage' a few times, but you guys are on a whole new level."

Diana: "Hahaha! No, sweetie. It's just us, though it is a universally held belief amongst our faithful that sex, IN MARRIAGE, is God's greatest gift to us, and it's an insult not to enjoy it, unlike some other faiths that mutilate their little girls because they think all pleasure is a sin."

Sierra: "What's this about 'being on stage?' Hmm?"

Chapter Six

ASHAMED, I TURN my eyes downward. "I've done a great many things that I'm not proud of when I walked the streets."

Sega: "Don't be ashamed, sweetheart. Confession and forgiveness of sin is a cornerstone of our faith. We won't hold your past against you, so if you feel like sharing your story, don't be afraid to do so. We just ask that you don't repeat it."

Sierra: "It would also be good if we have fair warning about any 'surprises' headed our way."

Alex interrupts our rather heady discussion by fidgeting nervously and shyly admitting that he liked our review of his "performance." Everyone's jaw hits the floor, including mine.

Sega: "Oh, dear. You've awakened a strange interest in our boy."

Atari: "Don't worry. When it's your turn, I'll be sure to cheer you on, properly!" There is a serious edge in her voice.

Just as sparks start to fly between them, Alex grabs them both in a big hug. "You guys are funny." And he starts to laugh with genuine mirth.

The rest of us can't help but join in as all the day's tension melts away. I can see now why everyone treasures his happiness so much. When he smiles, he lights up the room without even trying.

What we didn't realize at the time was that we weren't the only ones laughing. Of course, the audience at large got a huge thrill out of Alex's embarrassing admission. The one who got the biggest laugh, of course, was his own mother. In between fits of absolute hysterical laughter, she cried out, "That's my boy!"

Guard 1: "Knock it off in there!" <BANG> <BANG>

Guard 2: "Forget it. Don't get yourself worked up. She'll be 'punished' soon enough."

The matriarch, however, was NOT laughing. She wanted Alex (and us) to suffer. When she realized he was actually enjoying himself, she went absolutely berserk.

Matriarch: "He... he's actually ENJOYING IT!? He WANTS to be watched!?!"

She proceeds to grab a chair and uses it to try to smash everything in sight: computer monitors, keyboards, servers, microphones, control panels, nothing is exempt.

When an underling arrives to report, she locks onto her with a face that's a mask of absolute rage.

Matriarch: "YOU! Report, and it had better be good!"

"Madam Matriarch, the 'surprise' you ordered is almost complete; sometime near midnight, it will activate. The 'contestants' will get a rather nasty 'wake-up call.' One they're not likely to forget for the rest of their lives, short as they may be."

Matriarch: "Excellent. At least something is going right today. Deploy 'it' when ready, except for Mr. Udderweis and his ten 'friends.' I've got special plans in store for them."

"Understood." The underling then leaves the control room in a hurry.

Matriarch: "At last, Mr. Dolorean, you and your little pagan enclave will be 'erased' from the world."

Meanwhile…

We, who were completely oblivious to the scheming and workings of the matriarch and her willing stooges, were sound asleep, buck naked, but asleep. Suddenly I heard an all too familiar voice.

Voice: "Shiatsu… Shiatsu! Wake up, Shiatsu!"

Shiatsu: "Wha…? Wait, who's there!? Show yourself."

Voice: "You know me. Come. There is not much time."

Shiatsu: "You. I have not heard you in so long. I thought you had forgotten me. What do you want?"

Voice: "I have not forgotten you. Wake the others. You must be baptized. Your mind and soul need to be pure for the trials ahead."

Shiatsu: "Baptized? I know nothing of this faith. Why now? Why not tomorrow? Why not after the Games?"

Voice: "Trust in me. I will not lead you astray. Have you forgotten what happens when you ignore my call?"

Shiatsu: "No. I may not know the faith, but I know my husband and sisters; I will not let that happen again."

Voice: "Then wake them quickly, and do as I have asked. Their lives and yours depend on it."

The voice then goes silent and does not respond to further questioning.

Shiatsu: "Wake up! Everyone please wake up!"

Alex: "Shiatsu! What's wrong?"

Shiatsu: "We are not alone. I can't explain right now, but I need to be baptized. Please."

Sega: "Eh?! Why now?"

Sierra: "In the middle of the night?"

Diana: "Something doesn't smell right."

Shinobi: "You'd better have a good reason."

Shiatsu: "I've heard a voice. A voice I haven't heard in years. The last time I heard it, it told me not to join in a raid on the Street Scorpions, your gang, Shinobi."

Shinobi: "I remember that raid. It was a dark, dark night for both our gangs."

Shiatsu: "I ignored the voice, and we went ahead with the raid, since our intel came from someone whom up to that point was a trusted source. Turns out that 'source' was working for the matriarch elite and was giving us good intel to gain our trust. When we launched the raid, the Matriarchy was expecting us. Many of my friends died that night, and I wound up in a cell, undergoing many indignities before coming here."

Shinobi: "And I wound up at 'Exile Island' where I watched friends die until Ms. Dolorean bought me."

Shiatsu: "I have sworn never again to ignore that voice, and it's telling me that if I don't get baptized, right now, our lives are in mortal peril."

Sega: "Sweetheart, if what you're saying is true, then you may be more blessed than you can possibly know. Alex, get our formal wear. Atari, set up candles, or the best ritual illumination you can at the sauna. Diana, do what you can about the proper incense. Use mosquito repellant with citronella if you have to. Shinobi, take care of anything I may have missed. We're going to do this, and do it right. We may not get another chance."

Once the preparations are complete, Sega proceeds to purify the water in the sauna and bless it.

Sega (in Gaelic): "Glorious Gaia, mother of nature and source of the waters. We ask that you bestow your blessing upon our humble pool for the sake of the anointing and the cleansing of sin. In the name of the most holy, we beseech you. Please answer your servant's humble prayer, Amen."

The sauna water glows briefly and then exudes an aroma to match that of the citronella that Diana is burning. Atari could not find candles, so she had to rig a ring of flashlights around the sauna. Aside from these lights, the ritual is performed in darkness as using the room's overhead lights is taboo during the ceremony. Sega then enters the sauna, and kneels within.

Sega (in our language): "Will the applicant come forward?"

While the rest of us are formally dressed, I, Shiatsu, as the applicant, remain completely naked and walk forward to the sauna and after entering, I am asked to sit down.

Sega: "Who here speaks for this child?"

Alex: "As her husband, I do."

Sega: "Are there others?"

Everyone: "As her sisters in marriage, we do."

Sega: "Do you swear to protect and guide her as she learns our ways?"

Everyone: "We do!"

Sega: "Do you swear to teach her right from wrong, and see to it that she does not stray from the light to the best of your abilities?"

Everyone: "We do!"

Sega: "Do you swear to keep her away from the wiles of the Evil One and his many temptations?"

Everyone: "We do!"

Meanwhile, the matriarch was in a panic. Thanks to her rage-fuelled sabotage, the Games Network was broadcasting the baptism ritual. Broadcasting a non-sanctioned religious ritual is a crime punishable by death, both for the one who broadcast it, and for the audience watching. Of course, watching the Harem Games was mandated by force of law; failure to watch the Games was also punishable by death, and the burden of proof lay on the defendant to show she had good reason not to watch, ie, power failure, near-death illness, or something else drastic beyond the defendant's control had to be proven in court.

Refusing to watch on moral grounds (like watching the participants do something 'unseemly') was insufficient.

In other words, we unwittingly were performing the first live baptism ritual before the public in centuries, with the blessing of the matriarch's own Games broadcasting system, and the Matriarchy was powerless to stop it without killing every citizen of the Empire of the Goddess, including themselves.

Matriarch: "Control! CUT THE SIGNAL! Change to a commercial! Play music over the sound! DO SOMETHING!"

Control: "I CAN'T! Someone on your end has locked the transmission. I can't shut it off. It was YOUR orders that mandated we make it that way, so no one could hijack the broadcast by hacking into our networks here or your networks through us!"

Matriarch: "You!" (points at Martufe O'oharra who is also in the room) "Shut it down, NOW!"

Martufe: "I'd love to. I really would. I am a VERY law-abiding citizen of the Empire of the Goddess, but I can't. SOMEBODY has done a real good job of sabotaging the equipment here. I could call for maintenance bots to come here and repair/replace the components; in fact I already have, but that would take quite a bit of time. If you want to blame somebody for this mess, you should start with whoever did this." (Waves at all the damage and debris) "That person is the criminal here. I don't have a clue as to who did this; perhaps you or one of your staff does? When you find her, bring her to me, and we'll see about punishment, but there's nothing else I can do."

Matriarch: "You're enjoying this, aren't you?"

Martufe: "Absolutely. A non-sanctioned religious ritual being broadcast by the Harem Games' own network, which everyone is forced to watch, BY LAW, and nothing can be done short of having the Matriarchy kill itself? Bwahaha! I would have never dreamed something like this could happen! Oh, by the way, you can't blame Alex Dolorean or his girls for this either. YOU are the one who planted cameras in his room, started the preliminaries early, AND started the broadcasts without notice. He had no input whatsoever. Even if he had known, he couldn't do anything about it. Oh, and don't think about 'asking' me to cut the power either. Even I can't do anything about the facility's geo-thermal power source."

The attendant suddenly rushes in. "Madame Matriarch, 'THAT' is now ready for deployment."

Matriarch: "Finally, somebody competent. Deploy 'THAT' immediately. We'll shut down the ritual itself, with their deaths."

"Understood." The attendant runs off to do whatever the matriarch had planned.

Martufe: "Just WHAT are you going to do?"

Matriarch: "You'll see, and then it will be MY turn to laugh, Mr. O'oharra."

While all that was going on, we were just finishing the ritual of my baptism into the Christo-pagan faith.

Sega: "Shiatsu, have you come of your own will without compulsion or coercion?"

Shiatsu: "I have." (Sega pours water from the sauna over my head using a cup prepared earlier by Shinobi earlier.)

Sega: "Shiatsu, do you seek to renounce your past of sin and death?"

Shiatsu: "I do." (Sega pours water over my head again.)

Sega: "Shiatsu, do you swear to follow the path of our savior and his teachings to the best of your abilities?"

Shiatsu: "I do." (Sega pours water over my head again.)

Sega: "Shiatsu, do you swear to avoid the wiles of the Evil One and his many temptations?"

Shiatsu: "I do." (Sega pours water over my head again.)

Sega: "Now that you are free and cleansed from sin, do you swear to forsake the path of sin, and never return to your old ways?"

Shiatsu: "I do." (Sega pours water over my head again.)

Sega: "Then with the blessings of Gaia, the spirit of the Earth and bringer of water, and in the name of the Father, the Son, and the Holy Ghost, I welcome you, Shiatsu, to the fellowship. Husband, and sisters by marriage of this child, clothe and guide her from this moment on so that she does not stumble and fall back into the path of sin, death, and sorrow. In His Holy name..."

Everyone: "Amen!"

No sooner do I climb out of the sauna, and get dressed in my tuxedo, and everyone cheers, than a low rumbling sound can be heard, and the ground shakes beneath my feet. Everyone's eyes go wide. "Earthquake?"

Alex: "No. Too convenient. This is obviously today's 'surprise.' Of that we can be certain."

Sure enough, the room begins to collapse around us. All thoughts of fleeing into the hallway are abandoned, as the path to the door is the first to go. Next, the doorway to the bedroom shatters into splinters, which narrowly miss us. We see the bedroom crushed beyond recognition, but it isn't debris doing the crushing, not normal debris at any rate. Something that looks like a giant metal claw has stabbed each bed, and the space between the "fingers" of each claw is nowhere near enough room for a person. If we had been in bed just now, instead of performing the baptism, we'd all either be dead, or wishing we were. Suddenly, the feeling of free fall takes over, as if we're in an elevator that had its cable cut. We quickly lie down on the ground to minimize the damage. When we crash into the ground, what wasn't crushed before is certainly crushed now. The room is a total loss. Fortunately, the ceiling is thinnest over the sauna, and we were able to fend off the debris.

We quickly assess our situation, and miraculously, aside from being seriously shaken, and receiving some new bumps and bruises, we are undamaged. When everything settles down, we stand up and dust ourselves off. A dove lands on my head, and the voice calls out.

"This is my dear child, in whom I am well pleased."

This time, I'm not the only one who hears it.

Alex: "Did you hear that?"

Everyone: "We sure did!"

The audience at large is shocked and confused. "Did the dove just talk? What kind of power was that? 'This is my dear child' ...what does that mean?"

Alex's mother was crying tears of joy. "Oh, my dear Alex, you're blessed beyond blessed. You are married to an authentic anointed prophetess. You couldn't make me more proud if you tried!"

The guards turn, look at each other, and, with a look of absolute horror on their faces, cry out simultaneously, "Shit! This is what we've been afraid of! They're on the move! The Matriarchy must know, at once!"

At the control center, the matriarch drops to her knees, the wind completely taken out of her sails. All she can say is a hushed "No. This can't be happening. This just can't be happening!"

Martufe: (whistles) "An authentic anointed prophetess. Now here's an event that hasn't happened in thousands of years, and you've broadcast it, where everyone is forced to watch, by LAW. Your propaganda war against them won't hold up much longer. Oh, by the way, that 'earthquake' was a nice touch. Was that your 'surprise?'"

Martufe: "Sadly, you can't claim credit to it now because that would only be adding official support to a, and I quote, 'nonsensical pagan religion' despised by the empire."

The maintenance bots arrive and begin restoring the control center to full functionality, but the PR damage has been done. Everyone with viewing access has seen with their own eyes that the "truth" told to them about initiation into the Christo-pagan faith was all bald-faced lies. If one ritual was lied about, were there others? And what was with that dove, and the voice? The arena has no doves. In fact, doves aren't even native to the area where the training center is! So where did the dove that landed on the head of the prophetess come from? The rest of the Matriarchy scrambles for cover, running from the press, hiding their faces while PR agents say either "no comment" or a bunch of legalese that really doesn't mean anything.

Not knowing about any of this, we change out of our formal gear and into "hunting" clothes because we strongly suspect that our room is no longer part of the training center, and we have, in fact, been dropped onto the arena floor. It is no surprise to any of us when we find out that's exactly what has happened. An announcement comes over the arena loudspeaker.

"Congratulations on surviving the preliminaries, contestants! Due to technical difficulties, the 'outing' ceremony scheduled for this evening has been cancelled. We apologize for any inconvenience this might cause. Please make your way to the starting line within the time allotted. Failure to do so means instant disqualification." (In this case, disqualification means death by any means necessary.) "Happy hunting, everyone."

We soon see a fleet of shuttles heading out of the training area into the arena, obviously heading to the training point. "The fix is in now. It's so damn obvious, only an absolute idiot wouldn't understand. How does the Matriarchy expect to get away with it?"

Shiatsu: "Perhaps something has happened, something so drastic that they just don't care anymore."

Everyone looks around when realization hits. "You mean they broadcast us!? But that's crazy! Broadcasting an unauthorized religious ritual! Wouldn't they censor that, especially considering that people are compelled to watch the Games Network by law?!"

Shiatsu: "Maybe they couldn't for some reason. You did hear the 'technical difficulties' line, right?"

Alex: "Everyone. We need to hurry to the starting line, where those shuttles are headed. We should stay to the forests as much as possible; large open areas or trails are bound to be heavily trapped, and patrolled. If we weren't singled out for death before, we are now."

Alex: "And it won't be just Madam Ultrabitch anymore. We can expect every last one of the Matriarchy will be very busy trying to save face by 'erasing' us!"

We would have taken the heavy weapons we won earlier through great pains, blood, and sweat, but they're buried under a pile of rubble right now; and we can't spare the time to dig them out, as we don't know how long we've been given to get to the starting line.

We follow the shuttles as best we can, but it is rough going through a tangled jungle with a dense canopy that makes shuttle sightings a rare event. Still Alex was right about the open trails. We can easily see giant footprints in the dirt and hear loud roars heralding some very large predators. They can't get at us through the thick trees, but they know we're here too. Surprisingly, the shuttles never get too far ahead. Are they taunting us? No. They're having problems of their own; seems like the Matriarchy wants to gain the "benefit of the doubt" by having the shuttles trudge along as opposed to getting there easily. They DO still need that gambling income after all. We manage to avoid some traps in the jungle, thanks to Shinobi's sharp eyes, but I know those traps are nowhere near the true level of sophistication of which the Matriarchy is capable. This IS the twentieth time that the Games have run; they're not amateurs. I suppose it's just not "entertaining" to eliminate us too early.

We finally make it to the "starting line," where the shuttles descend. There is no surprise in any of us upon seeing Ash Udderweis and his ten flunkies with their harems emerge from them. As we suspected from the beginning, each has a full set, so that's 176 people.

A few moments later, Tendo Akaneda with and his harem appear. Like us, he has the minimum six, but for a different reason. It's not that he couldn't get more women, he just didn't want them. He has three that petitioned to be here, and three more that he supposedly selected at random, at least according to his dossier.

Kakizaki Ikari and his master, Arcades Allbright appear with six ladies each. Even if they could get more women, they don't want them. They are well-known misogynists. I secretly weep for the girls who got stuck with them, though I can't pity them too much as they are certainly going to try to kill us just so Mr. Allbright can get his "wish" and hopefully let them go. Though I suspect both of those men will be very happy in making them kill each other.

Several "neutral" boys with harems of all shapes and sizes from the minimum six to the maximum fifteen also appear. Seventy-five percent of the original contestants are gone.

Lastly, Mercedes Oberhorn arrives in the clearing, alone! Seems he sacrificed every single girl in his harem just to get here. Every last one of us is grateful that Alex, a man who truly treasures us, is our "king."

Before we can say anything, the shuttles take off on remote and begin scouring the arena for the fallen.

An automated announcement begins. "Congratulations on making it this far, contestants. Please stand by while the arena is reset and prepared." As corpses, or remains of corpses, begin being piled up like kindling in the shuttles by the automated retrieval bots, the announcement continues. "Fighting between 'kings' is strictly prohibited until clean up is completed, and kings have been assigned their respective castles. Kings who lack at least the minimum number of maid servants are exempt and will be considered disqualified if they remain that way after clean up is complete. Thank you for your cooperation."

This rule was made early in the history of the Games. It would allow those kings who reached the "starting line" without enough girls to raid each other for more, purely to entertain the Matriarchy and the audience. Let's say, as an example, there were two kings, one with five girls, and one with three. They would fight it out, and the winner would then have eight girls while the loser would be dead. This time Mercedes Oberhorn is alone in this status, so there's no one he can raid girls from. This doesn't stop him from trying; as he approaches us, as he grabs me…

Mercedes: "This is all your fault, peasant! You stole Shiatsu from me! She is my whore! You have no right to her..."

Smack! Alex slaps him right across the face! <SMACK> "That was for insulting her just now. THIS is for insulting her earlier, with interest."

Mercedes gets knocked on his rear with a wicked left hook.

Mercedes: "You... you HIT ME! You actually dared to hit me, TWICE!"

When Mercedes rushes at Alex to tackle him, Alex puts him in a choke hold. "DO shut up! It is entirely YOUR fault that you apparently did not take this tournament seriously just because the title has the word 'GAMES' in it, despite Martufe clearly admonishing us otherwise. I don't care what relationship you had, or THINK you had with Shiatsu. GET IT THROUGH YOUR THICK SKULL THAT SHE IS MY BRIDE! Fifteen beautiful girls are now dead, thanks entirely to YOUR negligence. I don't know how you were brought up, but my mother always told me since I was very small that a BRIDE is your ally in battle, your companion in life, and most importantly the mother of your children; as such, you treat her with the utmost respect AT ALL TIMES. You make sure to treat her better than you want to be treated yourself, and if you have ANY say in the matter, you don't let someone else treat her badly either. That being said, I really have no grudge against you; the only mercy I can grant is to make this quick."

Mercedes: "Wait, what are you..." <Crack!>

Alex rapidly twists Mercades's head, breaking his neck with a sickening crack. He then proceeds to dump the now lifeless body on the ground.

Moments later, a robotic unit flies into the area and approaches Alex.

Robot: "Termination of Mercedes Oberhorn by Alex Dolorean detected. Initiating investigation: Alex Dolorean, please identify yourself for the record."

Alex: "I am Alex Dolorean."

Robot: "Acknowledged. Did you terminate Mercedes Oberhorn?"

Alex: "Yes."

Robot: "Did you hear the announcement that 'king'-versus- 'king' fighting was prohibited?"

Alex: "The announcement excepted those 'kings' who had less than the minimum six brides. Mercedes had none."

Robot: "Accessing... Statement is correct. Mercedes Oberhorn had zero registered brides upon entry into the 'starting line.' This is clearly less than the required six. Contestant Alex Dolorean still has six brides registered. Contestant Alex Dolorean is still prohibited from hostile action."

Alex: "Am I not permitted self-defense? Mercedes was moving aggressively towards one of my brides. I moved in her defense."

Robot: "Processing video footage.... Acknowledged. Contestant Mercedes Oberhorn was clearly engaged in hostilities towards registered bride of Contestant Alex Dolorean, and then proceeded in hostile acts against Alex Dolorean directly. Contestant Alex Dolorean, we find no rule violations on your behalf. Please refrain from further hostilities until the starting ceremony."

Alex: "Acknowledged. Barring self-defense, I will actively avoid hostilities until after the starting ceremony."

Ash: "You stupid piece of junk! Alex snapped his neck." (points at one of his underlings) "YOU! Take out that piece of trash!"

When the underling moves to attack…

Robot: "Attention all contestants. You will receive one warning. Initiating hostilities against a referee robot or interfering with a ruling is a rules violation. This will result in increasing penalties up to and including termination of the offending king."

Chapter Seven

A HOLOGRAM OF Martufe appears directly above us. "As you have already noted, referee robots are now in the arena. They were originally designed to defend the arena against armed military-style invasion. They have far more range, agility, durability, and accuracy than the bots Alex defeated. In other words, attacking them is an exotic form of suicide."

Suddenly, the face of a new matriarch appears in the skies overhead. This matriarch wears a uniform very similar to the Peacekeepers, but the regalia in the collar and the medal on the chest are unmistakable.

"These referee bots were placed by OUR orders, Ash Udderweis! Matriarch Udderweis is detained, pending the outcome of a full investigation regarding several incidents occurring at the Games this year. If you were receiving an unfair advantage over your competitors, that assistance is over. You will have to proceed on your own merits from now on."

Matriarch UDDERWEIS!?! That explains so much.

"Alex Dolorean, our preliminary investigation finds you not guilty of seditionist propaganda. Under the rules of the Games, you are permitted any religious ceremony you wish, provided it does not contain or refer to cannibalism. It is the matriarch supervisor's duty to screen out ceremonies deemed 'offensive' to the population. Security footage at and near the time of your ceremony clearly shows you had no knowledge of the broadcast and instead fully implicates Matriarch Udderweis in sabotaging equipment to broadcast your activities without your knowledge or consent. Be advised, however, that from now on, your activities ARE being broadcast, and any activity from you that is deemed seditionist or slanderous to the Matriarchy will be swiftly and severely punished."

In other words, no Christo-pagan rituals, not even the "harmless" ones.

"In other matters, while the equipment is being repaired, there are to be no unnecessary battles. Each of you kings has been assigned a castle. Markers have been provided so that each of you can get to the correct location. I recommend you head there immediately; a referee bot will be sent with each of you to make certain there are no king-versus-king battles until after the repairs are completed and the opening ceremony is finished. Be advised that while the referee will prevent fighting between you, it will do nothing to assist you if you are endangered by the environment or wild beasts. Staying on alert at all times is recommended. Thank you all for your cooperation."

So the second day's "surprise" is still an option, huh? And this time, we won't be able to jam the controllers. Right now, though, we have no option but to do what this new matriarch said and head to our "castle."

Alex: "Let's go. There's nothing more for us here."

Ash Udderweis: "That's right, you'd better run, freak! I'll mess you up!"

Robot: "Contestant Ash Udderweis. Are you attempting to provoke conflict?"

Ash Udderweis: "Pah! Whatever! Let's go."

Once we're out of sight of the others, Alex starts to break down. "I... I killed him!" He starts weeping like a baby.

Sega: "Shh. It's all right. You had no choice."

Shinobi: "Indeed. That was an act of mercy. A brat like him couldn't survive even one day at Exile Island. That's where 'disqualified' players go."

Alex: (sniff) "Thanks, guys. Let's hurry. I'm sure something bad will happen if we take too long."

No sooner does Alex say that than our path is blocked by a T-Rex. The referee bot immediately flies away so it doesn't get caught up in the battle.

Alex: "Nobody move. It shouldn't be able to see us if we don't move. Sega, Sierra, focus on the legs; if we can tip it over, we can escape. Atari, Diana, focus on the head; if you can fry its brain, it's dead. Shiatsu, stay close; we may need to fight at close range, and I need you to watch my back. Shinobi, if you see an opening, run. We need you to scout ahead."

T-Rex: "Ghwaaarrrr!"

Shinobi: "But..."

Alex: "Listen. This T-Rex can't be the only hazard on the trail, and you are ill-suited for this battle. The opponent is simply too large for your weapons to work. If you find traps, disarm them. If you find cages, sabotage them. If you find other enemies, deal with them if you can; if not, return with the intel. Go! I believe in you."

Shinobi: (sniff) "I... understand. I will not fail you."

When the T-Rex charges, Shinobi dashes off into the woods. Everyone else scatters. Sierra and Sega try turning the ground under the T-Rex to mud/quicksand, but it's too quick. Amazingly, such a big animal has the speed and agility of a cheetah. Using their powers, they just barely escape being eaten instead.

Atari and Diana combine their powers to make a massive flamethrower and launch the flame right down the T-Rex's open mouth. All that manages to accomplish is to piss it off!

T-Rex: "HHHRREEEEE!! GWAAAHHHRRR!!!"

Atari and Diana get blown back by a swipe from its tail. "AYI-IEEEE!!!"

Alex doesn't even hesitate; he takes advantage of the opening while its back is turned and hamstrings it with a combination upward slash and cross cut. Not wanting to be left behind, I do the same with the other leg. The beast falls. We barely have time to deliver the finishing blow before two more arrive...

I, Shinobi, know that my husband and sisters-in-law are in a pitched battle, and I want to run to them, but he's right. The battle is ill-suited for me. I would just be in the way. Right now, all I can do is clear the trail for them so they can escape. There are no obvious traps, and a close check of the trail itself reveals nothing. It wouldn't make sense for such big animals as a T-Rex to travel this trail if it's loaded with traps of all shapes and sizes, but it would be foolish to ignore the possibility.

Going through the forest, it doesn't take me long to reach the end of the trail, and Alex is right once again. There are caged beasts of all sizes here. I don't arrive in time to stop two adult T-Rex from going down the trail, but there are numerous cages with smaller dinosaurs, "poison spitters," young T-Rex, and several others I can't readily identify. The one that's most troublesome is the one in back, an ankylosaurus-like beast. It's so huge, it hunts T-Rex. Unfortunately, I have to deal with these smaller cages first. If I try to go after the ankylosaurus first and the other cages open, I'll be trapped, killed, and eaten. Even though I don't care about my own life, if something happened to me, it would hurt my husband horribly. He deserves better than that. I manage to sabotage the locks so they won't open on all the smaller cages. Even though the "poison spitters" try to stop me with their venom, the goggles made for me earlier protect me. Sadly, I don't make it to the ankylosaurus' cage. Even if I did, the beast is so strong that it rips the cage door right off its hinges before it fully opens. How did they manage to cage it?! It takes all my skill and agility to escape into the jungle before the beast is upon me. "HSS!! RWWWEERRRR!!!"

It helps that the monster had to go through a gauntlet of smaller cages to get at me. Even so, it was a VERY near miss that I got out of its reach into the forest, and up into the higher tree branches. The trees are too big, and too closely spaced for it to get at me easily. I do get a good look, and it has a control collar. So THAT is how they caged it. When it turns to go down the trail to the others, I throw a shuriken and damage the collar. That's all I can do. If I can't even help in a fight against a T-Rex, I'm utterly useless against one of those ankylosaurs.

With the smaller cages trampled (and the dinosaurs inside them killed), I've done all the damage I can. I'm torn whether to go back to my family or keep heading towards the "castle." I decide to head towards the castle. Perhaps there's something there that will make a difference, a rocket launcher, a ballista, a trebuchet, something. No point in sending such beasts against us if there's no way to beat them.

When I get to the castle, I am horribly disappointed. There is nothing here useful against the ankylosaurus. There's a single tent, a sleeping bag, a hunting knife, some pajama clothing that has apparently been chewed by vermin, and some canned goods. What was the matriarch thinking? We were going to kill the dinosaurs by expired produce?

I hold my head and sigh to myself at the wasted time and effort, and rush back to my family, knowing that I'm likely too late to even give them a warning.

What I couldn't possibly have known, is that Alex and the others received much needed back up from his friends, the raptors and dire wolves!

I, Shiatsu, am analyzing the situation, and it's not good. It took everything we had to take one T-Rex down. Now there are two bearing down on us, Atari and Diana are on the ground, not moving after being hit by that tail swipe. Even if we were all able bodied, we can't outrun them. The forest is no refuge; the trees here are spread too far apart to stop them. Shinobi only managed to get away earlier because the T-Rex was busy fighting us. I don't blame her for leaving. She didn't flee out of cowardice, but because Alex asked her to, as a tactical decision, and it was a valid one. It wouldn't have been good to try fleeing down this trail without any intel on what we would find. I can only hope she's bringing back some good news, because we are desperate.

I blink and dire wolves are pulling Atari and Diana away from the front lines and taking defensive positions between them and the T-Rex. They're not the only good news. Raptors run right up to Alex and challenge the T-Rex on our behalf!

Alex: "Sega! Sierra! Forget the legs and feet. Go for the eyes. Try to blind them. We need to give our friends every advantage we can!"

The two nod grimly.

Alex: <Scay Lee, Mai Fang. Tell your people to hold back, and when I give the word, go for the legs. That is where the prey is weak.>

The raptors and wolves growl in agreement with whatever Alex just told them.

When the T-Rex start to charge, Alex cries out, "NOW!"

Sega and Sierra manage to blind one, but the other continues to charge unchallenged. We dive between its legs as it passes over us. Standing still now is certain suicide. While its forward charge and side stepping ability is truly fearsome, its cornering ability is absolutely terrible. We take advantage of this by running perpendicular to the charge, but with two of them, it's only a matter of time before they get us, even with reinforcements. The raptors are doing their best to try and hamstring the blinded T-Rex, but as if the T-Rex somehow anticipated their actions, they can't get close without getting cast aside by the tail.

Alex: <Get back from that one, go after the other.> "SEGA! SIERRA! You know what to do!"

Once again, Sega and Sierra try the tactic of turning the ground to quicksand under the blinded T-Rex. This time it works! The dinosaur's size is its own worst enemy. It sinks rapidly into the ground and drowns to death in the dirt.

We don't even have time to cheer this monumental accomplishment, as a new horror arrives to take its place. An ankylosaurus breaks into the clearing, howling with rage at us.

Raptors: <BIG FIN! We must flee!>

Wolves: <Opponent is too strong! We cannot win!>

Just when we think all is lost, we hear Shinobi's voice. "The ankylosaurus has a damaged control collar! If you can somehow lure the T-Rex close to it, you might have a chance!"

Alex: <We do not need to beat them. We just need to get them to fight each other!> "Sega, try to draw the ankylosaurus closer. Sierra, try to blind the T-Rex with a dust cloud."

They look at him perplexed, but they do as he asks. Sure enough, the blinded T-Rex smashes into the ankylosaurus. It doesn't like that AT ALL! It immediately goes after the T-Rex, and all hell breaks loose.

Shinobi: "The way to the castle is clear; run for it!"

We don't hesitate. I grab Atari and Alex grabs Diana.

Alex: <Everyone. Run. Flee while you can.>

The raptors and wolves scatter, and we flee to the castle while the ankylosaurus makes a meal of the T-Rex. We are just as disappointed in what we find as Shinobi was. There is nothing here that is useful against the ankylosaurus, and now that the control collar is broken, even the Matriarchy can't contain it.

Alex: "You did the best you could, Shinobi. It could have been far worse with all those other beasts there, and you managed to get us out of that alive. I'm proud of you." He hugs her and pets her on the head, a gesture she accepts happily. "Still, we have that ankylosaurus to deal with, and no way to do it."

Shiatsu: "A hunting knife? You've got to be kidding me. Even my smallest blade is better than that."

Alex: "Well, the walls are sturdy, so we can wait it out in here if need be, but that's not going to help us deal with it in the long run. And a hunting knife isn't really a good tool for cutting trees to make siege weapons or armaments."(sigh)

Shinobi: "Agreed. We need an axe, at minimum."

Sierra: "I'd settle for a needle and thread. Look at these clothes, plus one tent and one knapsack? It's probably infested with all sorts of insects too. I'm really wary of going into that lake to wash it, and our 'new' clothes, but I'm more afraid that something poisonous has taken a liking to them."

Sega: "I can go to the lake. At the very least, I can tell if the water is safe to drink. Alex, would you mind joining me? I will need someone to help me carry this... stuff, and watch my back."

Alex: "Sure. And afterwards, if it's safe, maybe we can go... swimming?"

Sega: (tweaks his nose) "I know what you REALLY mean by that, sweetie, and I'm flattered that you're finally taking the initiative, but we've got a lot of work to do. Plus Atari and Diana need to be checked on first."

Shiatsu: "There doesn't appear to be any internal bleeding, and from what I can tell, they just have a mild concussion. They should be fine by tomorrow."

Sega: "Well, that's one less worry at least. Alex, you really should have asked about them yourself, you know?"

Alex: "I'm… I'm sorry."

Atari and Diana: "It's OK. You got us here alive, and that's what matters. Just don't let us slip your mind like that again, OK?"

Alex: "Thank you!" He runs over and hugs them tight, crying in gratitude.

Shiatsu: "Alex, you can let go now; they need their rest, and the rest of us have work to do. Get that 'laundry' started."

Alex cheers up immediately, takes all the clothes and the knapsack to the lake, and starts washing with gusto. Sometimes I really wonder if he isn't just a little kid shoved into an adult's body. Well, that's what they love most about him, and to be completely honest, so do I.

It's a good thing he does so too, because the moment the clothes hit the water, insects and vermin of all types start trying to flee. Those that drown get eaten by fish. Well, there's fish in the water. That ALMOST qualifies it as safe to drink. At the very least, all the vermin and insects have been removed from the gear we have inherited. Sadly, water alone won't do anything for the smell, but he did his best. After seeing the vermin try to crawl out of the sack, he deliberately dumps it all in the lake and tramples it underfoot, just to make sure EVERYTHING drowned. The look of disgust on his face says it all.

Sega: "OK, dear. I think you've done enough."

Alex: "You sure?"

Sega: "Absolutely. Now take them to Sierra, and see if she can do anything with them while I test this water. Come back quick!"

Alex nods vigorously and does as he's told. What an interesting child. On the one hand, he leads us perfectly on the battle field. On the other, as I said, he looks to us for approval just like a small child. I could watch him all day, but I have chores of my own to do. Now that I'm certain Atari and Diana are in no danger, Shinobi and I start setting up the tent and, a fireplace, and we make camp here.

When the chores are all done, Alex happily brings to us the fish he caught. Sega wastes no time praising him for it and patting him on the head, all of which he accepts with a smile.

Sega: "Good news is there doesn't seem to be any large predator in the water. Bad news, there may be small predators like bacteria and parasites. I suggest we boil the water until we know for sure."

Atari: "Normally, I'd advise against lighting a fire when we know we're being hunted, but the enemy already knows where we are. I mean, there was a glaring beacon over this place already, so attempts at stealth are pointless. The problem is, what are we going to use to boil the water? We don't have pots or pans, and I don't particularly trust this 'canned food' that we have here."

Alex: "Oh, that's easy. Here's a trick Mommy taught me when we used to go camping together, just the two of us. Sierra, can I borrow the knife please?"

Sierra: "OK. Sure."

Alex takes a couple of the pieces of firewood that I've prepared and carves them almost into flutes, and some of the bigger ones, he carves into mugs. And after running to the lake and filling them with water, he puts them in the fireplace. "Now we just sit back and wait; in a few minutes, boiled, fresh water."

Sure enough, he's right. The "flutes" make excellent pot stickers, and even though the wood is in the fire, the boiling water keeps it from burning. Once the wood "mugs" are extracted, Alex simply says, "Now let them cool, and we have nothing to worry about."

After we set up the fish on sticks so it can cook, Sega pulls Alex aside and says "While we're waiting on that, how about the 'swimming' you wanted to do earlier?"

Alex: "You sure we have enough time?"

Everyone: "Go ahead. We'll save your share for you. Have fun!"

They remove their jerkins and then run and dive into the lake. For the audience at large, I'm sure it must look like skinny-dipping, but we know better. Once they get a bit farther away from shore, about waist deep or so, they take a standing position where the water's buoyancy takes a bit of the strain off Alex. They go about it fast and furious, as if they expect someone to "walk in" on them at any moment. We won't, of course, but considering where we are right now, it's a perfectly valid concern. They transition between positions quickly, some of which are physically impossible without the buoyancy of water. When they reach the finish, they do so in the classic "face-to-face" standing position, holding each other tight, at which point, and everyone cheers, including me this time. Atari holds up her hands with "1"-and-"0" signs on her fingers. Is she saying the performance was a perfect 10? They return to us completely disheveled, panting and soaked to the bone, but happy. Diana then proceeds to playfully pounce on Alex.

Alex: "Are you feeling better, Diana?"

Diana: "Pfft! As if I'm letting a little bump on the head and some bruises keep me from my man!"

Sierra: "Dinner's done, you two! Get it now before it gets cold!"

Diana: "Oh, pooh! And just when it was my turn to have some fun!"

Alex: "HAHAHA! You're fun!"

Sierra: "Come on, I'm sure you can have your 'fun' after dinner. Just leave some for me, OK?" She smiles with a wicked glint in her eye.

Alex: "Try to save the bones, everyone. We can't afford to throw anything away now."

I have no idea what Alex has in mind with fish bones, and looking at the other's faces, I see they are equally perplexed, but after Atari had us salvage the robot parts earlier, we are not in a position to complain.

When the cooking is done, before we eat, once again we perform the ritual blessing over our meal, only this time; we do it quietly, in case the matriarch finds this "offensive."

After finishing our meal, Diana playfully tackles Alex, and Alex happily goes along without resistance. I won't go into details about their lovemaking, but I will say this: Diana is a screamer. Her pleasurable moments are VERY loud. Nobody bothers to cheer after that. Diana had her own fireworks. When they're done, Sierra quietly and calmly simply states, "It's my turn now."

We now know Alex will get our powers this way, and doing so improves our chances, but that's not why we're doing this. We're not even doing this anymore because we want to give him children, although we do. No. We're doing this because very soon now, the Games will start for real, and we are showing our affection while we still have a chance. Sierra wrapped herself tightly around Alex, not letting him go until they were done.

Shinobi goes to him next. Her "afterglow" was stolen away by his traumatic outburst last time, and we felt it was owed to her. Initially, he enters her with her legs up his chest, and her feet around his head and neck, but eventually he moves into the "love swing" position and then the "reverse scissors" position. Now this is a position that needs to be entered with care as moving carelessly can cause serious damage to the man because his most sensitive part is bent the wrong way. In exchange for this risk, he gets to see all the action, and they both have much stronger climaxes, or so I'm told. While linking hands, his thrusts are short, but powerful. It's easy to see the joy on her face.

The finish was obviously VERY satisfying for both of them.

Shinobi: "I'm so happy! Thank you, everyone! And thank YOU, Alex." She gives him a huge kiss right on the mouth, and bounces away happily."

What happens next shocks me. All the others grab me, and gently strip me down. "Now, honey, it's your turn."

Shiatsu: "My turn, wait...what?"

Sega: "We know you're his first, dear, but what was done to you, both of you, is inexcusable."

Sierra: "If Shinobi deserves a do-over, you do too, and for a better reason."

Shinobi: "Yeah. You need to know the true joy of a man. You need to feel with your own body how wonderful it is, and that it's NOT meant to be a source of pain and humiliation."

Diana: "We'll watch over and protect you."

Atari: "Don't be afraid. We've got your back."

They all push me gently but firmly towards Alex. This time it's his turn to kiss ME. His hands caress me everywhere, from the sides of my face to the tips of my toes, and his mouth follows as if he's tasting me for the first time. Whatever resistance I had, just completely melts away. He gently holds my hands as he pulls me on top. After mounting him, he has me put my legs straight between his and then he wraps his calves behind mine, pinning me down. He wants to do the "scissors" position with me. I've NEVER done it in this position before. Not only is it hard to maintain, but the thrusts are shallow, and the climax tends to be weak. But the climax isn't what he has in mind. He is clearly communicating that he wants ME, not just my body. He gazes longingly into my eyes, runs his fingers through my hair, runs his hands gently over my lips, my neck, my breasts, my buttocks, and my belly. Even though I'm on top, he has almost total control of the action. I can lean back or lean forward, but that's about it. If I try returning his caresses, I risk losing my balance. With me, he's really taking his time. It's like he's telling me he doesn't want me to go.

Every once in a while, he has to thrust so he doesn't fade, but in the meantime, I really lose track of time. Was it a minute, a half-hour, an hour? I can't tell, and I don't care. He is making me feel exceptionally close, as if I'm an extension of his own body. I know I've never been like this before, but it just feels so familiar. It's as if I've forgotten a dear old friend whom I haven't seen in years. When the inevitable finish does come, he puts his head in my bosom, cries tears of joy, and for the first time ever, I hear those sweet three little words every girl dreams of, "I love you."

Shiatsu: "What about the others?"

Alex: "I love all of you, dearly. If something happened, I don't know what I'd do!"

Alex: "But Shiatsu, I really can't explain it. I feel like I've known you longer than all the others, as if we were together from birth. I can't get you out of my mind. At night I dream of you; when I wake, you're the first I think about. When I'm with you, my heart leaps for joy. When we're apart, even for a moment, I feel as if someone is trying to take you away, and it scares me. I... I don't want to let you go! I can't live without you! Please, don't let me GO! Don't leave me!"

He really starts crying in earnest, and holds me very tight.

Chapter Eight

SHIATSU: "IT'S ALL right. I'm not going anywhere."

Everyone: "Neither are we."

Diana: "That was beautiful."

Sega: "He's chosen his 'favorite,' all right."

Sierra: "That was like watching the sunset, nothing to do but just sit back and enjoy the glow."

Atari: "That confession was perfect. You couldn't ask for a more burning, passionate appeal."

Shinobi: "That fear in his heart is still there, waiting, ready to pounce."

Everyone nods in agreement. We don't know what kind of conditioning was done to give him such profound separation anxiety, but with his mind so fragile, we figure I should just lie beside him until the terror passes.

Atari: "Diana and I'll take the first watch."

Before any of us can complain, she says, "Yeah, yeah. Concussion.

I know. All I have to do is yell if something happens, right?" We can't really argue with that. We all agree that over the next twelve hours we should take four-hour watches in pairs, with Alex and me being last, Shinobi being a chaperone. Why Alex and me together? Not only am I the "favorite," but also being separated from him is far more likely to trigger an attack, and that could be fatal for all of us. Further, it's also a good idea to let him have a full night's rest first since that seems to be a requirement for assimilating our powers.

When our turn comes, I awake to find Alex already gone. Did he wander off in his sleep? Is he searching for me? Just before I start to panic, I hear the felling of trees. Shinobi and I go investigate, and sure enough, Alex has decided to do something very constructive.

Alex: "It's not good to have trees too close to the castle, makes it way too easy for people and things to sneak up on us."

I look back at the castle, and there's other stuff there that wasn't last night.

The walls are not brick and mortar any more, but smooth like marble, and at the very top where we sleep… is a stone ballista! We grab Alex and, drag him back to the castle, and have him explain himself.

Alex: "It just… came to me in a dream, and I had to try it out."

Shiatsu: "Try WHAT out?"

Shinobi: "Look at the ballista, closely. Do you see what I see?"

What I first thought was stone is, in fact, petrified wood! The bolts are petrified wood too!

Shinobi goes and wakes everyone. Thinking we're in a state of alert, everyone comes ready for battle only to see what Alex did, and is amazed. The castle is now ringed with six petrified wood ballista turrets, and ballista bolts. Covering our tent is an archery tower, and much of the trees that were close to the castle have been felled, and cleared away.

Atari: "How did you cut all the trees?"

Alex: "With this." He summons a steel flaming sword that cuts wood like hot knives cut butter, and then to quell the flames, he uses the other hand to summon a water fan.

Sierra: "What about the castle walls?"

Alex: "Oh, that was easy. I just closed my eyes, imagined it, and a little bit later, it was like that."

Diana: "What about everything else?"

Alex: "Oh, I got the idea in my sleep, took a few tries, but had plenty of wood to play with. It was fun."

So he doesn't just copy our powers, and our surface memories; he combines and enhances them. And he did all this for FUN?! In a few hours?! What a scary ability.

Shiatsu: "This is all great, but you could have let us know first. When I didn't see you this morning, I was very worried."

Alex: "I'm sorry."

He looks like he's about to cry, and then suddenly remembers something. "Oh. This is for you, Shinobi!" He hands her a handmade bow. It's very ornate, but the "string" is actually those fish bones Alex had us save last night. They'd been fused together into a highly elastic thread that won't break or cut easily.

This time, it's Shinobi's turn to cry. "It looks just like the bow I had when I was little. How did you know?"

Alex: "I don't know. It just felt right. Oh, here are some arrows too. There's more on the tower."

The arrows are very well made, almost as if he's been making arrows for years, but had stopped for a while.

Everyone: "We've never seen you make arrows before! Who taught you!?"

Alex: "I... I don't know!" His flustered face is so cute!

Suddenly a thought occurs to me, something I've only read about in sci-fi novels. "No. It can't be!"

Shinobi: (looks at me curiously) "Oh? What are you thinking?!"

Shiatsu: "He's reading our memories and skills from our RNA, and he's doing so unconsciously!"

Everyone starts to look at me perplexed, but then Atari speaks up.

Atari: "You're right. That does make sense. Our company's been doing research into that for years. A side-effect of that research is our popular V-R machines. Supposedly it allows you to transfer mastery over languages, arts and crafts, even fighting and weapon skills, from one person to another without training overnight. Unfortunately, unless the person receiving those skills trains them, and frequently, they are quickly forgotten. It would certainly explain why Alex suddenly 'knows' things that he didn't before he was 'intimate' with us."

Shinobi: "I don't really understand what you are saying, but the gist is, either he's going to need to practice everything he's learned, and practice hard, OR we are going to have to do 'that' with him every night, or both."

Going by the reflection in Alex's eyes, everyone's got this real mischievous, almost predatory look in her eyes, including me. Alex, perhaps feeling like a prey animal surrounded by predators, looks mortified. "I'm... I'm sorry! Forgive me." When he tries to run away, I grab him, pull him back to my chest, and hold him tight. "Shh! It's OK. We're not going to hurt you. You've done nothing wrong. You've just made us all VERY happy."

Alex: "Really!?" He looks up from my chest into my eyes.

Shiatsu: "Really. Just relax. We are not going to force you. We love you, very much."

Alex: "Thank... Thank you! BWAAAAHHHH!!!"

His tears of joy and overwhelming emotion remind us just how INNOCENT he is, and why we like him so much. They also remind us that he's not a machine built purely for OUR benefit. He's got feelings too.

He doesn't cry long. He pulls away and starts looking around. "We've got company!"

"HISSS!!! GWAAAEERRR!!!"

It's the ankylosaurus! There are far richer pastures, like Udderweis and his flunkies, and yet it's coming after us! That control collar Shinobi mentioned must not have been completely disabled. It may not be under control, but it can certainly be aimed. Someone has certainly aimed it well. It begins to charge the castle.

Alex: "Everyone, grab a ballista, except Shinobi!"

Shinobi: "Why am I special?"

Alex: (points at the archery tower) "Get up there. There may be something coming after the beast, and I need you ready."

Shinobi understands immediately and climbs up the tower quickly.

The beast stops just short of the walls and slams at them with its armored tail. Had they been left as bricks and mortar, they would have fallen, easily. After what Alex did, however, they are shaken but not broken, although even the strongest rock can't take too many more hits like that.

Alex is holding up his hand; it's certain we can't fire recklessly. That armored body would likely deflect even these petrified bolts that Alex prepared, and we can't waste them. Fortunately, he doesn't need to hold his arm up for long. Seeing that the blow with its tail didn't work, the beast rears back to either try to climb up or smash its entire weight into the wall. As soon as it wails, that's when Alex sends the signal, and we let all our bolts fly at once. Alex manages to get one right in its mouth. The rest of us have our blows bounce off, but they don't do so harmlessly. Since it was rearing backwards we knock it off balance, and it falls over backwards with a booming THUMP.

Alex: "Reload. Quickly! Its belly is exposed!"

He doesn't need to tell us twice. Even though the petrified ballista bolts are quite heavy, the ballistae are surprisingly easy to load. We finish loading them just in time, as the beast is rocking, trying to right itself.

We don't even wait for orders; we fire right at the belly. We turn it from armored lizard to pincushion. Even if it's not dead, it will be soon. Being unable to right itself, its own weight will crush its organs.

Shinobi: "In the forest! The beast was not alone!"

It isn't long before we notice the ones who were herding it, Ash Udderweis and crew.

I am Tendo Akaneda , and I'm too late. I never planned on occupying "my castle." Instead, my girls and I would have been using guerrilla tactics against Ash and his ilk, seeing how, combined, they vastly outnumbered everyone else. Seems like this was a good idea too. After seeing Ash's "strategy" in motion, I became ill at this guy's sheer cowardice. I don't know how he, or one of his thralls, did it, but somehow, he gained control of something that looks like a giant, meat- eating version of an ankylosaurus; and his group was using it to demolish the castles of other contestants, along with the contestants themselves and then looting the bodies. If the "enemy" somehow survived the initial attack, Ash would send one of his thralls to inflict "assisted suicide" on the victim. When the referee bot arrived, it would take the "criminal" aside, interrogate him, and inflict punishment. Since Ash rotated the role of executioner, all of the killers were punished as "first timers." This involved getting tased and tagged, but they were otherwise all right. They wiped out all the "neutrals" this way, including Arcades Allbright and Kakizaki Ikari.

I had hoped on arriving at Alex's castle and warning him, but as I said I was too late. Ash got there first, or rather the ankylosaurus did. Alex was strangely well prepared. Not only was the castle itself heavily reinforced against the attack, but in less than a day, Alex and his harem also managed to equip it with six heavy ballistae and an archery tower. This was more than sufficient to take down the ankylosaurus, but the real threat came immediately afterwards. Even a heavily fortified castle can't fend off an attack force that outnumbers the defenders more than fifteen to one. My girls want to rush to his aid; after all, they believe he would give them a much better life than anyone else, including me. (They've been watching how he treats his girls, and under the rules the winner gets to keep all the survivors if he so desires.) I want to rush to his aid too, but the old saying "You can't help someone if you're dead" rules the moment. "I want to help him, I really do, but they are many, and we are few. We have to pick our moment carefully."

When the flare went up, and the "ceremony" signaling the start of the true Games played out, Alex and his harem gave Ash's army a hell of a fight. Alex made no strategic or tactical mistakes. His orders and their use of powers were perfect. Ash's army could not approach the castle by conventional means, and even considering the tactical situation, Alex could have won handily; but Ash didn't use conventional means, he used cowardly ones.

Ash had his army pin Alex and his girls down with machine-gun fire while zip lines came down from the trees towards the archery tower. In a matter of moments, heavily armed and armored troops swept down upon them from above. Even Shinobi, who could still fire her bow, was ineffective in stopping them. Alex's entire group soon found themselves wearing control collars, tased, stripped naked, and taken away. Almost all of Alex's possessions were left behind. Looks like Ash doesn't even have the decency to simply kill them either. He wouldn't have his gang take them away unless he wants to sadistically "play" with them first.

Okabashi: "Why didn't we go help them? You know he's a 'brother' in your faith!"

Tendo: "Tell me how, woman! Can you point out a way to help without getting us all killed, or worse?"

After a long, heated argument, it is finally agreed that there was no "good" way to go to their aid. All we can do now is follow Ash's gang of thugs and hope to thin their numbers a bit before they reach Ash's "castle." No such opportunity presents itself. We shadow them the entire trip, but they all remain closely packed together like hyenas. Like hyenas, they also make sadistic "laughing" noises while formulating new and interesting "games" that they want to play with their new "toys."

After taking their "trophies" to Ash's castle, Ash has them chained to the walls. (Where did he get those?) He then has them awakened by having them splashed with something. I can't tell what it is from here, but I'm sure it's quite unpleasant as water doesn't cling quite that way.

Ash: "Wakey, wakey! It's not good for the 'guests of honor' to sleep through the party. Right, everyone?"

Ash's thugs: "Hehehe! Time to pay up for our missing limbs, girly boy!"

Ash: "Ah yes. Too bad, the teacher's pet here can't call out to Martufe, or maybe call out to 'Mommy,' eh?"

Alex's face takes on a look of pure contempt.

Ash: "Oh, my. I really don't like that look. Boys, do what you want with his girls, but don't kill them or rape them. 'THEY' want his kids, for whatever reason… Oh! I know. Girls, 'pleasure' him. It would be good to have backup in case something 'accidentally' happens."

OK, I admit, I'm a bit of a pervert. Make that a total raging pervert. But seeing a guy chained down and taken against his will like this makes me sick. I'm racking my brain trying to think of something, anything, to end this, but I can't think of anything that won't just get us all killed.

Meanwhile, Alex's girls are getting all sorts of bizarre tortures inflicted upon them. One is getting pelted by rocks, another is getting burned, a third is getting choked/strangled, the fourth is getting her head shoved in a bowl and pulled up again, as if simulating drowning, and the last two are getting foreign objects shoved into their most precious places.

Alex: "Let them go, you despicable cowards!"

Ash: "Eh!? Say something? Girls! Do it, use plenty of tongue; he likes being watched, you know."

What? What is he talking about? Has Ash been receiving video intel from the Matriarchy?! That's a serious violation! Wait, what's that sound I hear, some kind of humming?

Ash's girl: "What's with that look? We've been ordered to pleasure you. It's entirely your loss if you don't enjoy it!" She mounts him after he was thoroughly stimulated against his will, and begins to thrust.

Ash's girl: "Oh, yes! What a good boy!" (sniff) "Anyone smell smoke?"

That's the last thing she will ever say. The humming sound was an electrical charge building in Alex's body. It completely fries his control collar, and the girl who mounted him against his will gets bisected from her crotch to her head. Alex then phases through his chains, and, in a matter of seconds, completely disembowels all the rest of Ash's girls. I finally get a look at his face, and his eyes are definitely reptilian, slits for pupils and everything; his teeth are also razor sharp, and his hands are now deadly claws.

Alex: "Grrrawwwrr!!"

Ash: "Stop! I'll kill them! I really will!" He shows Alex a remote for the control collars.

Alex simply hurls a ball of lightning at Ash, tasing him and pinning him to the wall. "Stay there quietly for a while. I'll deal with you soon enough." Alex then looks down at the disemboweled girls screaming with terror in their eyes. "What's wrong? It's entirely your loss if you don't enjoy it!" Recognition spreads across their faces. They know they will not get any pity or mercy now. Not even the mercy of a swift death. Alex then takes the skull and spine of the bisected girl, in a way reminiscent of the first *"Predator"* movie, (Yes, they still distribute it.) and in sheer moments transforms it into a spear that he hurls at the two who were throwing stones and using a flame thrower on his girls. The two thugs die instantaneously. He rushes over to the ones who were strangling and drowning the girls, rips their hearts out, and forces them down their throats.

As for the guys who were object raping his girls, they got steel spikes shoved up their rectum, so hard, that the other end came out their mouths. Their deaths were slow and most likely VERY agonizing.

That's when it happened. He stopped being human and grew, three, four, ten, twenty sizes and became as big as a T-Rex; he transformed into an authentic steel-plated dragon! "RRRAAAEEEWWW-WW!!!!"

"Rush him! He can't take us all at once!"

Those that went after him in a large group found the ground beneath them transform into quicksand, and they drowned to death in dirt. Those that tried to flank him and attacked either got torn to shreds or stomped like bugs, literally.

Machine- gun bullets bounced off harmlessly, and those shooters wound up looking like porcupines as Alex fired armor-piercing spikes at them from his tail. Snipers who attacked from a distance simply had the air sucked out of their lungs. In this manner, Alex single- handedly obliterated Ash's army of 175 "followers" in a matter of minutes. With no followers left to hide behind, Ash became the center of attention for Alex's rage.

Ash: "I am Ash Udderweis, the son of Matriarch Udderweis; I will not be bullied by a Christo-freak…"

Alex pounds him into the ground, once, twice, three times! "I trust I now have your attention?"

Ash: "GHWAK." He begins coughing up blood, and most likely has numerous broken bones.

Alex: "I'll take that as a 'yes.' Now I only have time to say this once, so it would be VERY much in your interests to listen carefully."

After Ash Udderweis fails to respond, Alex continues.

Alex: "Mercedes Oberhorn, he was after me because in some twisted, self-serving, 'spoiled brat' logic, he presumed that Shiatsu was his 'property' and could not get it into his skull that she is my bride. I understand that. I don't approve, but I understand it. Your thralls were after me because they believed that if they bowed and scraped before you long enough, they might get out of this with their lives. They were quite wrong, of course; there can only be one 'winner' of these Games. You certainly aren't a misogynist like Arcades Allbright or his thrall, Kakizaki Ikari; you had the maximum number of brides. You can't even cite religious persecution because you didn't know my faith until very recently. Given the choice, I would have HAPPILY steered clear of you, yet you were always going out of your way to harass, intimidate, oppress, and assault me. WHY?"

Alex: "I just can't figure out what your grudge is! Further, since you have obviously been getting video to which the other 'contestants' were not privy, you must know that you commanded your thralls to lay hands on one of God's anointed prophetesses. Your actions are no longer forgivable. Normally, you would be brought before a tribunal, your guilt established, and your sentence determined. We don't have that option here. As her husband, the duty of your punishment falls upon me, and your guilt is obvious. So tell me what your grudge is. Perhaps if it's something really, really good, I might be able to show mercy."

Ash: (cough, cough) "You damn, suck-up freak! Always making good with the teacher, insulting me behind my back, trying to one up and humiliate me! I HATE YOU, and your peasant little cunts!"

Alex: "That's it? Your entire grudge boils down to seeing me talk with the teacher after class because I had a question? You hate ME because you were too stupid to take advantage of a resource available to EVERYONE!? And you, the resident expert on unfair advantage, trying to lecture ME on a PERCEIVED advantage would be quite amusing if it wasn't so infuriatingly serious. You are beyond redemption. The only punishment befitting you is one reserved for witches, warlocks, and all others who fornicate with demons, devils, and other abominations for their own power and wealth. I will have to remove your seed from the Earth, BY FIRE!"

Alex then picks up and drops Ash on the other side of the castle wall, outside. What happens next is a sight that chills all our bones. Alex inhales an enormous breath and breathes fire, not just any fire either, but an increasingly hot fire. First Ash begins to blister, then his skin begins to melt, and he starts drowning on it. "Yaaarghglghgghglggh!" Eventually it reaches the point where his very bones burn, and the ground beneath him turns to lava, erasing him without a trace.

Alex: "I would say Ash to ashes, and dust to dust, but even that doesn't exist of you anymore." Suddenly Alex looks around, as if to see who is watching, and then proclaims while staring into a camera (which is supposed to be invisible to us), "MATRIARCHY! I know you're watching, and there are just three things I wish to say to you."

"One! You had better be prepared to return my mother to me, alive and well, as promised, or nowhere in the world will be safe for you."

"Two! You lay your hands upon my brides again, for any reason, and you will find yourselves neck deep in blood, your own."

"Three! From now on, no matter what happens, no matter what schemes are hatched, no matter what plans are made, no matter what traps are set, YOU WILL NOT GET YOUR HANDS ON MY CHILDREN! EVER! Take THIS as proof of my resolve."

There's that humming again. This time, though, the electric arcing is very visible. His wings are upright in a V formation with electricity arcing between them; the power just keeps building and building until an ion beam fires into the sky. A massive electrical and seismic shock wave rocks the entire arena. What we learned later is that the ion beam was enhanced by Earth's magnetic field and the Van-Allen belts, so when the beam reached the communication satellite in geosynchronous orbit over the arena, the satellite was completely obliterated. "Control," who was on the satellite monitoring the transmission, and controlling the control collars on the wild beasts, and now on Alex's girls, is dead. The collars fall off harmlessly.

Most of Alex's mass falls off in metal scales, like a snake shedding its skin. He hurriedly runs over to administer emergency first aid to his girls. Crying, all he says is "I'm sorry" over and over.

First, he frees the two girls who were being "drowned" and strangled. Looking at the throat of the one who was strangled and seeing her vocal cords were crushed, he just cries. Turning to the other, he proclaims, "Sega, are you OK? I need your help... for them." She nods, looks in his eyes, and after a brief cough, says "I'm fine. What do you need me to do? What about Diana?"

Alex: "Diana cannot answer." (sob) "Her throat is crushed. As for what I need you to do, can you use your powers?"

Sega: (Gasp) One quick look at Diana proves Alex's assessment. "I... I guess."

Alex: "OK. I need you to wash and prepare bandages, LOTS of bandages, while I work on the others."

While Sega starts tearing up the clothing on the corpses, and sanitizing it, Alex begins working on the others who were being object raped.

Alex: "Oh, Shinobi! They were violating you with the very present I gave you! I'm sorry, but this is going to hurt!" Alex begins removing a bow from between her legs.

Shinobi: "HNNNGG!!!"

Alex: "It's OK! Scream if you have to. Just try to relax. Don't clamp down or hold your breath. That will just make it worse." Shinobi, with tears of pain in her eyes, nods, and after rubbing her head a bit, Alex starts again.

Shinobi: "YAAAAAAHHHH!!!" Pant, pant. "AAAAIII-IEEEEE!!!!!"

Alex: "Good girl. It's out. I don't see any bleeding, but we're going to need to take you to a doctor soon. Don't move. I've got to go to

Shiatsu now." Alex dissolves the chains and lies her down gently.

Shiatsu (I guess) is in even worse shape; she's got all sorts of sharp implements shoved up into the holes between her legs, and has shallow cuts all over her body.

Alex: "Oh jeez! I don't even know where to begin! I can't just pull those things out. That could cause far more damage than when they went in!"

Sega: "I've got as many bandages as I can carry! What do you need me to do?"

Alex: "Start wrapping Atari VERY gently. Those bandages need to go on just tight enough to keep from falling off, but NOT tight enough to stick to the skin. Just from a quick look, she's got burns over 70 percent of her body, and just putting the bandages on is going to hurt, A LOT; but we can't leave her alone or she'll get infected, and that would be fatal. Now, Shiatsu, I need you to hold real still…"

Shiatsu: "I know. You're probably 'borrowing' my skills, right?"

Alex: "I… don't know. I just know that I'm NOT going to try pulling them out. I'm going to try 'absorbing' them very, very slowly."

Shiatsu: "OK. You might want to have a second set of hands ready just in case I start bleeding."

Alex: "Hehehe! I don't have that power."

That's when we arrive at the scene.

Tendo: "Perhaps we can help?"

Alex and Sega turn and eye us suspiciously. "Much as we NEED your help, the 'Games' has us as enemies, and we've got good reason to suspect you're up to something. What do you gain out of this?"

Tendo: "That depends. Just how far are you willing to go for our help?"

While Alex looks at me confused, Sega and my girl, Okabashi, understand my intentions immediately. Neither takes it well.

Chapter Nine

OKABASHI: (PULLS ON my ear.) "Forgive our perverted 'husband' here, but we genuinely want to help, and considering the energy blast earlier, it's likely the cameras aren't working; so we should consider the 'Games' are on a commercial break of sorts, and 'they' don't want us trying to kill each other right now."

As confirmation, a badly shaken referee bot approaches.

Bot: "D—...d—..due to unfo- ...for-...forseen technical, dif...-dif..., difficulties, remaining contestants will return to their neutral castles immediately. Non-compliance will not be tolerated."

Tendo: "We are rendering emergency medical assistance. They can't move right now."

Bot: "Scanning... stand by... critical injuries detected. Your claim is acknowledged. Do not attempt any hostile action. Medical bots have been summoned. Proceed with rendering medical aid. When complete, await further orders."

Tendo: "I get it. Laguna, could you help Alex with … Shiatsu was it? Panama, would you mind trying to find something to help the burned girl with her pain?"

Laguna and Panama: "Got it!"

Panama: "Oh jeez! Simple aloe and aspirin isn't going to cut it here! We're going to need something much stronger to numb the pain and start healing." She begins using her power to scan the local area for useful pain- and burn-relief herbs.

Laguna: "OK, I'm here as your extra hands, Alex. I'll try to stop the bleeding, try removing those things."

Alex: "Thanks." He begins trying to "absorb" one of the blades in Shiatsu. "I'm curious, how long have you guys been nearby?"

Laguna: "Quite a while. We wanted to help you against Ash and his thugs, but just couldn't figure out a way to do so."

Alex: "I understand. I don't blame you at all. You wouldn't have been able to help us if you were dead."

Laguna: "Our 'husband' kept saying that. So it WASN'T cowardice on his part?"

Alex: "I don't know your husband, but yeah. I wouldn't have gone charging in blindly either."

Alex finishes "absorbing" the first of the daggers, and Shiatsu starts bleeding.

Laguna: "My turn, stand back a bit." She touches Shiatsu's abdomen, and the bleeding stops.

Alex and Laguna continue this for a while until all the visible implements are removed. They surprisingly have good chemistry, much better than I had with her. Maybe it's the situation, and he's just too worried to be embarrassed, but he doesn't seem to be too concerned about being naked in front of strangers.

Panama doesn't find anything within her range that would help, so I ask Virginia if there's anything in her seed kit that would be of use.

Virginia: "Let's see, cherries, raspberries, blueberries, some mint, peach pits, an avocado pit, chamomile seeds… CHAMOMILE. That might help. If nothing else, it will help sedate her a bit."

She picks a nice place and uses her ability for growing plants rapidly to grow a patch of chamomile grass, and a raspberry bush. "I figured we could use the berries for a bit of flavor. Can I have some water, please?"

Sega: "Sure." As she goes to water the plants…,

Virginia: "Oh not for me, Monica. You're up."

Monica: "Sure thing." She pulls a pot out of her back pack and then adds the chamomile and raspberries to it. "Some water here, please." After Sega adds some water to the pot, Monica uses her "cooking" powers to make perfect chamomile tea with raspberry flavoring. "Here, have her drink this. What's her name?"

Sega: "Atari. Her name is Atari."

Monica: "Beautiful name. OK. Have Atari drink this tea. It will help her sleep while Laguna tries to help stabilize her. That's all we can do for now."

Alex: "Thank you, everyone."

Suddenly he collapses. Seems he's reached his limit. The medical bots arrive, stabilize everyone else's condition, and then analyze Alex's condition. "Anemia and iron deficiency, severe. Blood type O negative." Makes sense, all those steel scales had to come from somewhere. He receives a small blood transfusion from one of the packs the bots brought with them, just enough to stabilize him, and then we receive orders.

Referee bot: "Contestant Tendo Akaneda, use the provided stretchers and move Contestant Alex Dolorean and his brides to his castle. You may continue to provide medical and humanitarian assistance, but any hostile action prior to the resumption of the Games will be punished with deadly force."

Sega: (slaps her forehead) "I can't believe we forgot about Sierra! I admonished Alex about that earlier! Medbot, how is Sierra?"

Medbot: "Inquiry acknowledged. Bride designated Sierra has a mild concussion, multiple contusions, and lacerations consistent with sustained light blunt force trauma. Direct medical intervention is not required."

Sega: "Thank God. Now I owe Alex an apology, but first I'm getting dressed even if I have to pick random clothes off of corpses. I don't like the feeling of SOMEONE'S eyes on me."

Damn it. She noticed. I was hoping to enjoy the view a bit longer. Alex is one lucky guy; his girls are all so perfect, perfect!

Monica: "Yes, let's get them ALL dressed if we can. There's some 'Roman' eyes here."

Tendo: "Oh, come on! Is it that bad?"

Everyone: "YES! It is!"

In a hurry everyone gets covered up, except for Atari who is burned from head to toe, and can't be covered, but there's nothing sexy about second-and third-degree burns. Once the girls are unchained, and the unconscious and immobile are placed on stretchers, we begin moving to Alex's castle. It takes two trips, but none of them are left unguarded; or alone with me. Guess I'm not really trusted. (Sigh). I really wanted to see if Alex's rack is real, purely for the sake of scientific curiosity, of course. I mean, I've heard of men with breasts before, but either they were obese, or if there actually was breast tissue, like milk ducts, the breasts were small. Alex is obviously a guy, but those are double Ds if I've ever seen them. Barring implants, how did that happen?

Sega: "No, they're not implants. He's VERY sensitive about them, and if you go near them, WE will never forgive you."

What? Is she telepathic too?

Sega: "No, you're just VERY easy to read. Don't think you'll fool any of us. Furthermore, Alex is INNOCENT not naïve. Don't try to trick him. He won't like it."

Well, at least it's a nice place. There's plenty of fresh water in the lake and, there's obviously fish; someone built a campfire, and the archery tower makes for a decent roof, while there's also a tent with a knapsack.

There's plenty of room for everyone. When it's time to turn in, Alex winds up with his girls at the knapsack and tent; my girls take the area under the tower. I get sent to the roof. "First, you sleep alone. We don't trust your 'Russian' hands. Second, your gunnery skills are more useful up there."

Atari winds up near the tent because it's just too painful to be under covers. A makeshift tent is made over her. The chamomile tea wears off soon, and she begins moaning in pain with heavy, labored breathing. Sega, unfortunately, is far too exhausted to move, and Laguna's healing abilities have hit their limit as well. Still, I keep watch, and about half way through the night, something very weird happens.

Shiatsu, who shouldn't be up and around, is standing, wearing a pure white gown, and glowing over Alex. But wait, a closer look shows that's not Shiatsu. Shiatsu is still lying in the knapsack with the others.

"Hello, Alex, my good and faithful servant. Your wrath today was well justified, you even avenged my chosen vessel, and yet you still seek forgiveness. This pleases me greatly. As a reward, I will grant you one wish. Simply name it and it is yours."

Alex: (sob) "Please, stay with me. Don't go away."

"HAHAHA! You surprise me, young Alex. You could have wished for wealth beyond measure. You could have wished for long life for yourself and your family, as well as many children. You could even have wished for death upon your enemies, and I would have granted it gladly for their wickedness has reached my eyes, and ears, and its stench sickens me, yet they are desperate in it. Instead, you wish for me to remain by your side to guide and protect you. So be it. I will neither leave nor forsake you, and as long as you seek my voice and heed my teachings, all that I have said and more will be added unto you. As proof of my word, I will ease this child's suffering."

The glowing image reaches its hand out to Atari, and she glows for a moment; then the labored breathing and the moaning stop, replaced with a normal, gentle breathing rhythm and the rapid eye movement associated with normal sleep.

"I have made her body whole again, but you will have to heal her heart and mind."

The image then touches Diana's lips. "Let not slander, profanity, or needless guile pass these lips, lest a worse fate fall upon you." Suddenly Diana's throat glows for a moment then fades.

"Instead sing happily unto your husband and unto The Lord, and both you and your husband will not only be blessed but also be a blessing on nations."

Suddenly, the image turns to me. "So it seems you still have enough faith to see me and hear my voice? As you stand now, the only thing you can do is choose a successor, and that is only because of your office. There is much sin in your heart. It would be wise, if you value your soul, for you to confess and repent while there is still time, but that time is short. I should not need to say this, but Alex is not yet ready to fully see and hear me, nor is it yet the time to reveal myself unto the world. For now, say nothing about what you have seen tonight. That is my only command to you."

The image then kisses Alex on the forehead. "Even if you forget everything else that happened here tonight, remember this, Alex. The time may come when I need this vessel to do my holy works. Treat her well and impede her not." It vanishes, leaving Alex sleeping peacefully and happy.

The next morning, Atari awakes and everyone is shocked at her miraculous recovery. Diana even sings with joy at both her and Atari's recovery, and it is the most beautiful sound I've ever heard.

Laguna, to her credit, quickly rejects the praise aimed her way, saying that her healing powers aren't nearly that strong, nor has she ever undertaken such an enormous and complicated task. When I am interrogated because I was on watch, I, remembering the admonition, honestly say that I can say nothing about it, except that the two girls who recovered have a very healthy glow, and it is a shame that Alex is missing this. Alex would continue to sleep, unable to wake for the next three days. During those three days, while the Matriarchy tried to fix the "unexpected technical difficulties," they replayed both my story during the Games, and Alex's. DAMN, has he been seeing a LOT of "action!!" I'm so jealous!

When Alex awoke he began speaking of having a strange dream, until he got a good look at his girls, saw what remained of their wounds, and said, "So it wasn't a dream. All that happened, and I did those horrible things. You guys must hate me! BWAHHH!!!!" He began crying in earnest.

Sega: "Shh! We don't hate you. I also owe you an apology. I admonished you for forgetting about Atari and Diana's concussion earlier, and then I go and forget about Sierra while you're wearing yourself out taking care of us."

Sierra: "That's right. You just did what you HAD TO in order to protect us. You can't be showing mercy when outnumbered 176 to one and your family is being horribly tortured before your eyes."

Shinobi: "Don't forget. They were violating you too without pity, and forcing us to watch. They brought it on themselves."

Atari: "If you hadn't done what you did, I certainly would have died. You have nothing to be ashamed of. It is good, however, that you are not proud of what you did either, and keep that part of yourself on a very short leash."

Diana: "In short, we are not going away any time soon."

Alex: "Thank you, everyone. You are all so good to me! Sega, you can admonish me anytime, even if you make the same mistake yourself later. Just as long as you realize and correct it. Shiatsu?"

Shiatsu: "What I have to say can and probably will offend you, offend all of you, but it has to be said. So everyone, please don't say or do anything until I'm done. It's going to be hard enough as it is."

Everyone settles down for a long, and possibly annoying speech.

Shiatsu: "Alex, when we first met, I was sent to you as your whore, not your bride. I was sent only for the sake of collecting your seed. Since that failed, I was ordered to take your children, by subterfuge or by force. When you learned of this, it would have not been surprising if you looked upon me with hatred or contempt. Instead, you rushed forward to protect my body, my virtue, what little of it remained, and eventually even my soul without asking for anything in return. You have introduced me to five absolutely wonderful women who have been nothing but generous and kind to me, including Shinobi who should have had good reason to hate me, and when we made love, it was in the most gentle and intimate way possible. There is absolutely no doubt in any fiber of my being that I am your most precious person. Even though my soul belongs to almighty God, my heart, my mind, and my body are all yours, now and forever. I, absolutely, am not going anywhere. Woe be onto anyone who tries to take me."

Tendo: (whispering) "Are you recording this, Okabashi?"

She nods happily in agreement. All my girls have stars in their eyes. They're really eating this up. Even I'm getting a bit misty eyed.

Before anyone can say anything else, Shinobi speaks out.

Shinobi: "There is something you need to know about me, Shiatsu. I'm not with the Street Scorpions anymore, nor will I ever be with them again. I learned firsthand that you were right to fight them. These people I once called my family proved themselves nothing more than brutal thugs. When I was a member, if I wanted anything from them, I had to pay a price, and they paid a price for mine. That's what I thought 'family' was. After being 'bought' from Exile Island by Alex's mother, I learned different. Alex and Ms. Dolorean were ALWAYS glad to help me in anything, without asking for anything in return, so did his childhood friends. Being raised on the streets, this made me very suspicious. 'Free' could get very expensive, very quickly."

Shiatsu nods in understanding.

Shinobi: "But it really got to me when my old 'friends' found me and tried to take me away. At first, at the VERY first, I thought, 'At last, freedom,' but nothing could be farther from the truth. They wanted me to kill Alex and his mother and help them rob the place blind to set up as their new headquarters. Of course, I knew if I even tried, I would be executed immediately, but they didn't care. They only saw me as a purse to plunder. They even looked at the clothing provided by the Doloreans with unbridled greed and envy in their eyes. When I refused, and cried out for help, Alex completely ignored the danger and ran to my aid. Outnumbered and with no powers of his own, he still came to help."

Shinobi: "He was soundly beaten until his friends arrived. You KNOW they had powers, and were they ever angry. After my so-called friends got their tails handed to them, Ms. Dolorean arrived. She stated in no uncertain terms that if they ever approached me again for any reason, or if they so much as darkened the door to our house with their shadows, she would have them arrested for messing with her 'daughter' and her 'daughter's slave,' and the punishment for that is being sentto Exile Island. Ms. Dolorean ALSO pointed out that the chances of being 'bought' there by someone as kind and generous as herself or Alex is virtually nil. Needless to say, I never saw them again, and now I know what family is. I have no reason to hate you, Shiatsu. Everything you've ever done to me, or I to you, was only self-defense. Besides, it is written 'Vengeance is MINE sayeth the Lord.' By accepting you, I now have five of the best sisters-in-law that a girl could ever dream of, and a husband worth dying for because he truly treasures me for who I am, not for what I can do for him."

Alex: "You are all so wonderful! Thank you for accepting me. It's a debt I can never repay!"

"Just keep being good to us, and that's more than payment enough."

Wow, now that's serious loyalty both ways. After hearing all that, I decide it's time to make my proposal.

Tendo: "Alex. There is something I need to discuss with you."

Alex: "What is it?"

His girls suddenly look at me with suspicion in their eyes.

Tendo: "When the Games commence again, I propose we duel one-on-one without involving our harems. Winner takes all."

Everyone gasps at that, and ALL the girls now look at me suspiciously.

Tendo: "I may not look it, but I DO care about the happiness and well-being of my ladies. The Games require you and me to fight, but not our girls, right?"

Alex: "That's true."

Tendo: "The Games also say that the 'winner' claims all surviving girls by default, right?"

Everyone: "Can't argue that."

Tendo: "What I REALLY want out of this, is, if you win, I want my girls treated right, and you've shown you can do that. So please take them as your brides in that case."

Alex: "All right, I promise that if I win, that I'll respect and protect them as if they're my brides, but whether I'll 'take' them as brides, depends on them, and my wives."

Sega: "Considering our conditions, I don't think any of us can argue against your proposal, Tendo Akaneda. So IF you win, we'll abide by the rules of the Games, and we'll abide by the rules of the Duel; but be on notice that after what we've seen you do, and seen you NOT do, we will not serve you. Alex could ask us with his last breath, and we will not serve you. God could open the heavens, come down in a tower of fire, and command us with an earthquake, thunder, or a mighty wind, and we will still not serve you. If you were to literally become the last man on Earth, and making children with you was a necessity to prevent the human race from becoming extinct, we would STILL not serve you."

Tendo: "You are right. Alex, I'm not worthy to have fine women like yours. I've been watching the 'highlights' broadcast across the arena with interest. I've been in the same situation as you on day one. My church, which was also my home, was stormed by the Elite."

Tendo: "While you were bound to a hospital bed, I was free to move. While you had one hundred stitches in your stomach, I was able bodied. While you smote that soldier and sent her into the hallway, bloodying a matriarch in the process, I did nothing. While you had to be tased to become 'compliant,' I surrendered quietly. The only reason Okabashi, Laguna, and Panama came with me is because if we didn't agree to come to the Games, the Elite boasted that we were all to be violated, tortured, and executed. Considering what you went through, I bet 'they' had that in mind for us anyway. I chose Monica, Zori, and Virginia because they had talents that would help our team in guerilla warfare. I thought this option was our best bet to defeat power blocs like the one that Ash Udderweis set up. You, on the other hand, had a handful of very close and very powerful girls with powers that could adapt to almost any situation. You probably could have beaten Ash in a straight-out fight, but what happened in your battle was being outnumbered, outgunned, outflanked, and overpowered. Now rest and gather your strength because when it comes time to duel, although I want you to win, I won't hold back. If you hold back, I'll kill you."

Alex: "Likewise. In a different time and place, we probably could have become friends. You could have easily killed us after what happened to Ash and his flunkies. Instead, you chose to come help us. You could have left us here alone and helpless. Instead, you stayed with us and helped us recover. You could have done any of a hundred different things to us, yet you, for the most part, acted decently and challenged me fairly as a true warrior. I have no intention of holding back, although that 'dragon' thing took too much out of me. I'm not likely to try that again anytime soon."

We both laugh happily at that statement.

Tendo: "Yeah. I don't think either of us wants that."

Now, no longer needing to be wary of being forced into battle against each other, the girls begin introducing themselves.

Okabashi: "Pleasure to meet you. My name is Okabashi. The 'Games' erases our family name. My ability is manipulating light and sound. I can do all sorts of things, including 'record' and 'playback.' My specialty though works over long distances. Provided I can see it, I can make a distant fight scene look and sound like it's happening right next to you."

Sega: "So you were watching us…"

Okabashi: "Only to try and find an opening. We didn't want or need to see 'that.'"

Sega: "As you're aware, I am Sega, and I have power to manipulate water."

Laguna: "As you know, my name is Laguna; my power involves

accelerated healing. I can only make wounds that would heal by normal means heal faster, and it costs me a great deal of stamina doing so. Let's be friends, OK?"

Atari: "Hello, my name is Atari, yes, THE Atari of the VR 'love' machine company. My power is controlling, f... fi... fire."

She begins shaking uncontrollably. "It hurts. I can't!" Her face becomes a mask of terror.

Alex grabs her waist and holds her tightly. "It's OK. I'm here..."

Atari: "NO! Keep it away!" She begins flailing around.

Alex holds her hands. "Shh! It's OK. We're not going to let it hurt you."

Atari: "It burns! NOO!!!!"

Sega splashes her with water and then runs up and holds her. "We're here, we're watching, and we won't let it burn you."

Eventually Atari calms down. "Thanks, everyone. It... it's so scary!"

Alex: "We're not letting go, until you feel safe again." Atari starts crying.

Sierra: "Those bastards. It's good for them that they are dead. Making her terrified of her own powers, it's as bad as making her afraid of her own body. She can't even say the name of her element anymore. Oh, I'm Sierra, Mistress of Earth."

Panama: "I'm Panama. I can find anything I envision within a certain range, whether plant, animal, or mineral."

Monica: "Hello. I'm Monica. I can 'cook' anything I envision if I know and have the ingredients. For example, if I have milk, sugar, cherries, and salt, I can put them in my pot here and make ice cream."

Alex: "Now THAT is a useful skill."

Monica: "Hehe! Thanks."

Diana: "I'm Diana. I have mastery over wind and air."

Virginia: "I'm Virginia. I can manipulate plant growth."

Zori: "Hello, sempai. I am Zori. While it doesn't work on living things, I can change anything I hold in my hands at the molecular level. For example, I can turn a coal briquette into a diamond."

Monica: "While that power may not seem like much by itself, just imagine the possibilities of combining it with mine."

Shinobi: "Unlimited ammunition…"

Monica: "For starters, yes. I'm sorry, you were?"

Shinobi: "I am Shinobi." She taps Shiatsu on the shoulder. "This is Shiatsu. We both summon iron weapons but use them in different ways. I specialize in projectile weapons like shuriken while she specializes in melee like swords."

Meanwhile, back at the training academy…

Matriarch: "Unbelievable. That Alex Dolorean actually destroyed a satellite in orbit, deliberately. Sadly, he will NEVER lend us his strength, thanks to YOUR stupid, petty, vindictive little agenda. The best we could hope for is that he will merely TOLERATE us and leave us alone. His mother IS all right, isn't she?"

(Former) Matriarch Udderweis: "What should I care about her? She deserved whatever she got. How dare she humiliate me before the others! Claiming I'm a fraud and so on."

Matriarch: "Ms. Udderweis, you ARE a fraud. You claimed your son was a direct descendant of Martufe O'oharra. Ms. Dolorean merely discovered the truth of the matter during a routine scan of his DNA after his 'contribution.' She brought it before us AS SHE WAS REQUIRED by law. Your punishment was something you brought upon yourself by your own lies! If Ms. Dolorean had NOT found you out, someone else would have. Furthermore, YOU brought your son into the Games yourself, and YOU forced Alex to be here. We're not even going to mention the matter of his sister. Our only hope of being 'tolerated' was his mother being returned to him, unharmed, as YOU promised. If his mother is NOT returned, he will come after us. I have no doubt about that. Nothing we've got can stop him as he is now."

A technician arrives at the office where the matriarch, the former Matriarch Udderweis, and Martufe are waiting. "Reporting as ordered, Madam Matriarch."

Matriarch: "Please tell me you have good news. We can't keep the Games on hold much longer. The audience is becoming restless. It's been three days since the 'incident,' and our cover story concerning the broadcast satellite is wearing thin."

Technician: "Indeed, we have good news. In just a matter of minutes, the news communication satellite will be within transmission range of us. We have permission to use it for the broadcast of the Games. It should stay within range for roughly thirty minutes before we lose contact for another twenty-four hours."

Matriarch: "We can thank the Goddess that there's only two 'contestants' left, Alex Dolorean and Tendo Akaneda. We can market this as a climatic final battle. Bring up a timer; I need to make an announcement so we don't waste any of this transmission time. After that, you're dismissed."

Technician: "Yes, Ma'am!"

Timer: 10:00 minutes and counting.

Matriarch: "Personally, Ms. Udderweis, if it were up to me, you would be on Exile Island right now, as an inmate, so you could know first-hand what a slave feels like. I'm also certain there's quite a few slaves there who bear a genuine grudge against you, and it would be quite fitting for you to know how it feels to be the target of a grudge, without an unbreakable shield of power and authority to hide behind. The Matriarchy has instead decided to have the winner of the Games decide your fate. Considering the fact that Alex Dolorean is deemed the likely favorite, I guess the others believe that offering you as a sacrificial lamb would appease him. I honestly don't know which fate would be worse for you. I recommend that you pray to the Goddess or whatever idol you worship that the winner is feeling merciful at the time. Oh, wait! You are your own Goddess. You have a problem, a serious one."

Martufe can't help but chuckle at the last two sentences of the matriarch's lecture. The matriarch then gets a microphone from the control panel and makes an announcement. "Attention contestants, attention. This is an urgent Games message. A timer has been activated to give you a chance for final preparations before battle. When this timer reaches zero, you will have thirty minutes to decide a victor. If a victor is not determined in that time, the referee bots will decide the contest by random chance. As I mentioned earlier, I strongly do NOT recommend trying to fight them. They can target and kill you long before you can even see them. That is all."

The timer now reads 8:45 and counting.

Chapter Ten

Tendo: "What? This soon?!"

Alex: "Looks like we've got no choice then. Either we fight or the 'referees' decide it for us."

Shinobi: "But Alex, you are not ready. Not even close! You JUST woke up from a three-day coma!"

Shiatsu: "Shinobi, he knows that, we know that, THEY know that, but the Games must go on."

Diana: "NO!"

Sega: "Alex's main problem is anemia and iron deficiency. He can't summon weapons right now, but Shiatsu and Shinobi can give him some."

Tendo: "Yeah, girls, my ammunition, please."

As the clock ticks down, both sides prepare for battle, not wasting a single second. While I check my twin guns, make certain everything is in working order, and put on my ammo belts, Alex and his girls prepare him with a dagger sash and equip give him twin swords that Shiatsu summons from her arms. Alex has to bend down and take them because she can't stand at the moment, considering her injuries.

Even though he looks a bit shaky, I can't afford to hold back. I'm sure 'they' will find some way to 'penalize' us if I do. I bet Alex is thinking the same thing. As the clock reaches the single minutes, he checks his outfit for fitness and his gear one last time, and then it changes into the seconds...

Ten... nine ... eight ...seven ... six ... five ... four ... three ... two ... one ...

"Commence fighting, gentlemen. May the best man win."

I waste no time lining up a shot, but he blocks a single bullet aimed at his head with his sword.

The next shot is at his legs, and he blocks that with his other sword. How is he reading my moves? I switch to semi-automatic mode, and when I fire, he's gone. I turn just as his sword nearly gives me a new haircut. "Fwish!" HOW does he move so fast, especially with all that weight on his chest?

Alex: "You REALLY shouldn't be thinking about that right now."

I manage to avoid most of it, but he still manages to cut my arm. Is he telepathic? DAMN! I swing up the gun in my other arm, and he knocks the gun away, nearly slicing my hand off in the process. I then take a punch to the jaw that sends me reeling. As he prepares to thrust his sword into my heart, I try to counter by raising my remaining gun at his chest. He spins around the other arm and again nearly takes my head off. I dive to reach my gun. He counters by using a throwing knife to impale the hand reaching for it. "Yarrgh!"

Having no choice, I roll away just as an overhand chop comes my way. It misses my vitals, barely, but it does catch my back as I roll. In return, I start firing short bursts randomly in semi-automatic mode while rolling away.

When I come to a stop, and try to get my bearings, he is on me in a second, attacking from the side. He tries to thrust a sword into my lungs, and I try to grab his throat with the hand that has a knife stuck in it. He ducks and rolls and lashes out at my legs. I fire straight down, hitting him in the shoulder.

Alex: "Ouch! That was good. You obviously have SOME training."

Tendo: "Right back at you." I take the opportunity to remove the knife from my hand, and throw it to the ground. My aim with thrown weapons is terrible, and even if it wasn't, he could read my throw a mile away.

We begin to circle each other, looking for an opening to exploit. I notice we're now surrounded by raptors and wolves. They seem to be just watching the fight, waiting for a victor, perhaps?

Alex: <Do not interfere. This is an Alpha fight.>

Wolves: <We know, furless cub. We wait and watch.>

Raptors: <We can eat prey?>

Alex: <No! Loser must be marked to prove Alpha. If loser eaten, mates will leave.>

Raptors: <Mates good. We not eat, for now.>

I have no idea what they are saying to each other, but even with that "Doctor Dolittle" act, Alex never once takes his eyes off me. Seeing him pant, I raise my gun to fire, but never get the chance. In a heartbeat, he coils up like a snake and leaps sword first upward at my chest, just a little beneath my sternum and right into the heart. It's over.

Tendo: "You've won, Alex. Now it's time for you to return the favor you owe me for coming to your aid."

Alex: (pant, pant) "Say it. I'm all ears."

My vision begins to fade to black. "Come closer, I don't want 'them' to hear."

He comes closer and then kicks the gun away, and puts his sword to my throat before lowering himself down close enough to hear me whisper.

Alex: "Mommy told me never to approach a wounded opponent as if he were dead. Now tell me what you want for this 'favor.'"

I, Alex Dolorean, have just won the "final" battle of the Games. Tendo Akaneda, the closest I've ever been to being friends with a boy, lies dying before me. He says that he wants me to return the favor I owe him for his saving my girls and watching over us. When I'm close enough, and have made sure there is no trickery involved, he whispers something to me. He's telling me his "wish." It's a wish I entirely agree with, and one I'll be more than happy to ask for.

Alex: "Rest in peace, Tendo. Your wish is now my wish, I promise."

He breathes his last, smiling. I close his eyes, and then I cry like I've never cried before.

I look up and his brides are crying too. Even though their relationship with him certainly did not seem as close as mine with my brides, they obviously cared for him too.

Alex: "Sierra, he needs a funeral. His brides deserve no less." (sniff). "Unfortunately, we can't erect a monument here."

Sierra: "Don't worry. He will, at least, get a tombstone."

I gather up his other gun; put it in his "free" hand, and cross his arms over his chest as I've been seeing in funerals for boys ever since I was very small.

We all gather around his body as Sierra begins the last rites.

Sierra: "Here lies Tendo Akaneda. We did not know him very long, but he had traits that would have made him a good friend, if not a good husband and father. He was loyal, generous, kind, and fought both with bravery and with honor. He could have won these Games by any number of cheap and cowardly tricks, yet not only did he come to our rescue, but he also proposed and dueled in a manner befitting a true gentleman. He will be missed. Does anyone else wish to say some words for the departed?"

Okabashi: "He was our husband. He may have been perverted beyond reason, but he still cared for us in the end."

Laguna: "He wasn't just my husband, he was my brother. We really didn't have much choice being here, but even though his thoughts were less than pure, he never tried to take advantage or force us. Good-bye, Tendo."

Panama: "He once saved Okabashi, Laguna, and me from a fate worse than death. Although I hated his perverted nature, I never hated him. Good-bye, husband."

Virginia, Zori, and Monica all speak together: "Even though he made it quite clear, frequently, what he REALLY wanted from us, we do owe him our lives because no one else was willing, or able to claim us. For that, we are grateful. Tendo, may your journey in the next world be a good one."

Sierra: "If there is no one else, then we hereby return this body to the earth from which it originally came, ashes to ashes, dust to dust. We wish your spirit a safe voyage in the next life."

Sierra opens the ground as a grave, buries him, and moves a stone into place as a marker over his head.

I touch it and use my powers to carve upon it the words "Here lies Tendo Akaneda, husband, friend. Rest in peace."

Just before the timer runs out, referee bots swarm over us, confirm Tendo's death, and the announcement declaring me the winner is voiced loudly over the intercom, with a large display on the dome covering the arena. I am quite certain that all the viewers back "home" are getting the announcement too.

When the announcement ends, my friends the raptors and wolves scatter, and I immediately think something is wrong. We don't have to wait long. One of the same hover cars that brought Ash Udder-weis and his gang of thugs out to the "starting line" approaches us. When it opens, I see the new matriarch greet us.

Matriarch: "Congratulations on your victory, Alex. That was quite the show. I'm sure it won't be forgotten. Everyone, please get in. You have all earned a full twenty-four hours of rest and relaxation at the training center before the awards ceremony tomorrow."

Even though she said, "Please," the tone of her voice, the look on her face, and the postioning of the referee bots around us indicate that this isn't really a request.

Alex: "We are honored that you came to us in person, Madam

Matriarch. We will gladly accept your kind invitation." Even though my tone is polite, and my posture neutral, it's obvious to my girls that I don't trust her as far as we can throw her.

Matriarch: "Excellent. We will certainly make sure that all your medical needs are met as well."

Alex: "Thank you."

Shiatsu has to be carried in, but the rest of us board the hover car. When we reach the training center, we are taken to the medical bay where the treatment begins. My shoulder is fixed up, good as new. As for the girls, they are all given a clean bill of health, physically, except for Shinobi and Shiatsu. They remain in the med bay while we meet with the matriarch at the office.

Everyone: "TWINS! They're both carrying twins!?"

Matriarch: "Yes. Shinobi should have no problem with the delivery. The uterus, cervix, and birth canal all look perfectly normal. Was THIS really removed from her, without tools, utensils, or help of any kind?"

The matriarch is holding the bow I carved for Shinobi.

Alex: "Yes, it was."

Matriarch: "Mr. Dolorean, you must have the hands of a surgeon. How you could remove something like this in that manner without causing damage is a minor miracle. Speaking of miracles, do you have any idea what happened to Atari? I've seen the footage, and even taking into account Laguna's abilities, there's no way for her to recover like that."

Alex: "With all due respect, Madam Matriarch, the only one who might have seen anything is now dead."

Matriarch: "That's certainly true. It's a real pity. There are many burn victims that could use some of what Atari got. As for Shiatsu, I have grim news. Please realize that I'm not blaming anyone present. You all did the best you could under the circumstances. Alex, may I call you 'Alex?' This is not going to be pleasant. Please have a seat."

It is decided that we all should sit down.

Alex: "You may, Madam Matriarch."

Matriarch: "Thank you. Now, Alex, what those thugs did was truly barbaric, and the damage was severe. Her cervix and birth canal are a total mess. You and Laguna are to be credited for removing the majority of sharp implements without further injury, but the real problem is the landscape left behind."

We are all shown an MRI of her pelvic area, and the sight horrifies us.

Matriarch: "As you can see, there's shrapnel of all kinds in there. Seems those goons broke off pieces of blades, rocks, any sharp in-strument they could find before you could stop them. Furthermore, what you can't see on here, is that the 'tools' you did remove safely left rather deep cuts that are only partially closed, thanks to La-guna's abilities. It's fortunate Shiatsu has been completely bedrid-den for three days, plus the trip here, and is now lying in a hospital bed. Had she been walking at any time, they could have all opened at once causing major hemorrhaging and death. In this state, she most certainly would not survive delivery, and the babies' chances are also quite poor. At the very least, she's going to need surgery to get the shrapnel removed, and ever since the 'outbreak,' delivery by C-section has only seldom gone well. YOU were delivered that way, Alex, but your mother lost her uterus in the process. Our options are very limited. Even if you were thinking of an abortion to save her life, which I know you are not, considering your faith, I would still advise against it since all the known techniques would have a very high chance of killing her as well. An artificial womb won't work either; we have to run some more tests to be certain, but it seems your would-be children are linked to her womb at a genetic level."

Alex: "In short, you're saying we need to find someone with a womb who has a very close match to Shiatsu and move the children there?"

Now even if abortion was an option, it would be abhorrent to us. My faith taught me that life begins at conception, and my mother always taught me that anyone who claims abortion is some sort of "right" because the woman can do whatever she wants with her body is clearly deluding herself. The analogy she gave me is like saying a landlady has the "right" to kill "inconvenient" tenants at will because she can do whatever she wants with her house. Even decades before the outbreak, medical evidence backed up that analogy. Fully formed children were slaughtered in the womb in the millions either by deluded, desperate, or irresponsible girls, or by force of law like in China, and still many "intelligent" people claimed that anyone opposed to the practice was just stupid, crazy, or bigoted against women.

Matriarch: "Yes. You are quite correct. Unfortunately, Shiatsu has a very… unique DNA, and I can't think of anyone who would match her."

Alex: "What's so 'unique' about her?"

Matriarch: "That's classified. I'd love to tell you, I really would, but the Matriarchy would kill us both, and our entire families if I were to even give you a hint. Your mother would have been ideal for the transfer, but as I said earlier, she lost her womb long ago."

Wait, did I hear that right?

Alex: "Madam Matriarch. You said my mother was ideal, but weren't we looking for a match for Shiatsu?"

Matriarch: "Yes... Wait, you can't be serious."

Looking at our confused faces, she suddenly realizes that we are.

Matriarch: "By the Goddess! This is far darker and deeper than I was told, or even thought possible. That Udderweis woman RE-ALLY did it, didn't she? Just how far back does her petty vendetta and its tentacles reach?! I'm sorry, Alex. I really am. I can't say any more about this until I've done some serious research. In the mean-time, you now have some serious questions to ask FORMER Ma-triarch Udderweis, questions that I'll happily compile for you, and I've been instructed to tell you that, as the winner, you have the duty of deciding her fate because of her OBVIOUS role in the attempted desecration of this year's Games. The evidence, ALL the evidence, will be broadcast tomorrow at the awards ceremony. Get some rest, everyone. You're going to need it. I'm going to break the news to Shinobi and Shiatsu, both good and bad. You should find your quar-ters restored by now. Go there and get some rest."

I, Martiarch Eldrorado, watch Alex and his girls leave to head to their quarters. I know Alex is many things, but stupid is not one of them. No matter how much he distrusts me, such distrust is well justified; he's not going to disobey my orders without good reason, and I have given him none. After I make sure they're gone, I head to the medical bay to see Shinobi and Shiatsu who are still lying in their beds. My arrival is met with understandable surprise.

Shinobi and Shiatsu: "Madam Matriarch. Why are you here? And where are the others?"

Matriarch: "Please don't get up, especially you, Shiatsu. There are some very important things that we have to discuss, alone. First, Shinobi, I have some very good news for you. Your husband's field treatment was masterful; there's no injury or trauma to you, but you need to remain here overnight for observation just in case, because the news doesn't end there. You're pregnant, with twins."

Shinobi: "I... I'm PREGNANT!? I'm going to be a mommy! SQUEEE!! I'm going to have Alex's babies! This is the best news I could ever have! THANK YOU!"

She truly begins crying tears of joy. THIS is the part of my job I just can't get enough of. Much as I want to bask in the glow of Shinobi's beaming joy, it just makes what I have to announce next all the more painful.

Matriarch: "Shiatsu, your prognosis is not that good. Alex and Laguna did their best. Considering they had no tools, implements, or assistance, their performance was exemplary, but you have severe vaginal and cervical trauma.

While I'm sure you would be overjoyed to hear that you are also pregnant with twins, this news certainly complicates things to the extreme. Considering the level of trauma, while you could carry them to term, the chances of a safe delivery are nil for both you and your children."

Shiatsu: "No... NO! You don't mean I have to..."

Matriarch: "I wasn't even going to consider mentioning abortion. Any and all methods available would certainly sterilize you, or worse, kill you from severe, unstoppable bleeding. Now, we are trying to find a suitable match for a surrogate who could carry your children to term and deliver them in your place while you recover from the needed surgery to correct the damage. In order to succeed, I need to ask you some serious questions. No matter how confusing, please answer them to the best of your knowledge."

Shiatsu: (sniff, sob, shudder). "OK. Go ahead."

Matriarch: "Shiatsu, do you have any sisters by blood?"

Shiatsu: "No."

That's not surprising. "Prior to the Games, have you ever met any of the Dolorean family, or Alex Dolorean?"

Shiatsu: "No, I haven't. I thought we were looking for a surrogate for me, not him. Does this have something to do with the fact that they're his children?"

Matriarch: "Yes, it does. I am not at liberty to elaborate right now, but the father's bloodline is very important in this."

Shiatsu: "OK. Please continue."

Matriarch: "Can you tell me anything about your mother?"

Shiatsu: "Not really. All I know is that I was thrown into the streets like trash by a Peacekeeper captain who told me my mother never wanted to see me again. That was three years ago. I've been on the streets since then, until now."

So Matriarch Udderweis really did it. Shiatsu's existence wasn't just erased in the records; she was erased from everyone's minds, including her own.

When she wasn't of any more interest, she was just dumped on the streets until Matriarch Udderweis wanted to go after Alex Dolorean himself.

Shiatsu: "I have a question. If someone from the father's blood-line would work, have you considered examining Alex?"

Matriarch: "What? Alex is a boy. He can't carry children!"

Shiatsu: "That's not entirely accurate. Alex is a hermaphrodite. I've examined him. I know. Granted, having a vagina doesn't guarantee having a womb, but we should check to be sure."

I am completely thunderstruck by this revelation. An honest to Goddess hermaphrodite, no wonder Alex has special powers and abilities while no other boy EVER investigated has. We are not entirely sure why some girls have super powers, it's not entirely a hereditary trait, but boys never had, at least not until Alex. This Shiatsu obviously has apprenticed under a medical practitioner at some point. It would be nice to meet her "master."

Matriarch: "You've obviously had medical training at some point. Who did you apprentice under?"

Shiatsu: "You might not have heard of her, Notoria Elderbairns. She took me in and trained me, until the Peacekeepers took her away. I don't know what happened to her after that."

No WONDER Shiatsu turned to a life of crime, and became the boss of the Street Vipers. If you can't live by honest means, you're going to live by dishonest ones.

Matriarch: "You've given me quite a lot to think about, and research that needs to be done. In the meantime, just rest there quietly. Any unnecessary movement could reopen your wounds."

When I'm done consoling her, I head back to the control room and summon Martufe O'oharra.

Martufe: "You called me, Madam Matriarch?"

Matriarch: "Indeed. I'm going to be blunt, as I'm sorely pressed for time. I know you don't like me. I know you don't trust me. I can't really blame you. Your encounters with the Matriarchy have been considerably less than pleasant. That being said, I don't particularly need your trust or approval. I DO, however, need your total cooperation if Shiatsu and her children are to be saved."

Martufe: "Saved? What do you mean? You have designs on them? As part of my duties, I've received genetic info on both Alex and Shiatsu, and suffice to say, they are of particular interest to me."

Matriarch: "I suspected as much. Further, since this is your facility, I can't exactly say, 'That is none of your concern.' I can say that Matriarch Udderweis has made a real mess of things, and I need to clean it up, starting with making sure both Shiatsu and her children survive. That's not going to happen using any kind of conventional methods, medical or otherwise, even though this facility has the best medical equipment in the world."

Martufe: "So what do you need from me? Can't you get what you need from the Matriarchy?"

Matriarch: "No. First, as I said, I'm pressed for time. Second, I don't trust the Matriarchy any more than you do. They've kept me in the dark about way too much 'need to know' information. Do you have any guards you can trust?"

Martufe: "I wish I did. The 'guards' are on record as utterly failing their duties, on several occasions. I'm going to need to 'clean house,' and find some better people."

Matriarch: (sigh) "I was afraid of that. For right now, the medical bay is on total lockdown. Nobody but you or I can get in there. Alex is well guarded by his girls, and as we saw in the Games, that's more than sufficient for right now, but we're going to need better guards soon. For right now, though, what I need are a secure terminal, my eyes only; all the documentation, records, and information you can give me about Alex Dolorean and Shiatsu; and any recordings of examinations he's been given."

Martufe: "That's a tall order. Can you at least tell me why?"

Matriarch: "Certainly, provided this room is secure." Martufe indicates that it is. "As you are no doubt aware, all documentation surrounding Alex and Shiatsu prior to the Games has been tampered with. What you may not know is that their memories have obviously been altered as well, including the memories belonging to Alex's childhood friends who are now his brides."

Martufe whistles loudly. "I still don't understand how any of that relates to Shiatsu's pregnancy."

Matriarch: "I've been informed Alex is a hermaphrodite. I need confirmation of this. Further, the children need a womb with a genetic signature VERY close to Shiatsu's, or the complications will be severe, possibly fatal. An artificial womb is not sufficient. I'm sure you know why Shiatsu's mother is not an option."

Martufe: "That Dolorean woman is something else, eh? Certainly would be a historic occasion. It would be the third time that I know of where a 'man' gave birth."

Indeed, there were two other occasions on record, at least that I'm aware of. On the first occasion, a hermaphrodite legally registered under the gender "male," impregnated himself with his own sperm twice; both children were happy, healthy hermaphrodites as well.

On the second occasion, a woman underwent gender "correction" surgery, legally changing her gender to "male" but keeping the uterus and ovaries, married a woman, and had two children through artificial insemination. When asked on *"60 Minutes"* if he realized people would be offended, he went and said, "Why?"

Cultural note: It should be stated that the "same sex marriage" movement was very strong at this point, and this "man" was clearly insulting both those in the group who were for the concept and those in the group against. The newspaper editorials towards him were not kind.

Now knowing what he knows, Martufe happily complied with my requests. The room was made ultra secure, and the terminal, to the best of his ability, is now "my eyes only." The documentation concerning Shiatsu and Alex is as disappointing as expected. There is NOTHING there concerning Shiatsu's family history, and Alex is listed entirely as an only child to Ms. Dolorean. There is also no record of Alex getting any kind of medical examination that would confirm or deny the existence of a uterus. I don't bother using the terminal for looking up any information regarding Alex or any of his brides. That would surely alert the Matriarchy and send all sorts of red flags my way. So instead I check on Notoria Elderbairns. If any alarms are raised about her, I could claim it is a legitimate inquiry regarding some old case work that I did not get a chance to complete before coming here. This is certainly true enough. I WAS pulled from my office rather quickly and without warning when the "baptism" scandal broke. I was specifically chosen because I was the only matriarch on the tribunal board for the trials of both the now Former Matriarch Udderweis and Former Matriarch Dolorean during their respective cases, and was trusted to be "impartial." In regards to Notoria Elderbairns, I have good news. She is still alive. Her medical skills are so well recognized that she was put in charge of the infirmary at Exile Island even though she's an inmate there. She's one of the few inmates "not for sale" and recognized as "national property." I would love to have her brought here and questioned, but my cover story about "legitimate inquiries" will only go so far. And bringing attention on her would only put her life or her mind in serious jeopardy. Since I can't think of anything else to do, I turn in and prepare myself for sleeping the night in this office, the only "secure" place available here knowing full well that tomorrow is going to be hectic. I couldn't have dreamed how hectic, or that Alex himself would bring the solution to the mounting list of problems I would face.

Epilogue

THE FOLLOWING MORNING, we all met in the cafeteria and began mapping out the schedule of events for the day. All supposedly ending with the broadcast of Alex's wish and his decision on what should be done about Former Matriarch Udderweis when the news satellite's orbit puts it in transmission range.

First on the list, of course, is Alex's exam. Alex is none too keen on the idea. I am told in no uncertain terms EXACTLY what his last "exam" was like at the hands of the Matriarchy, and I am appalled.

Matriarch: "That was unconscionable, even if it was to gather your 'contribution' to the gene pool or to collect a genetic sample. Matriarch Udderweis went too far! Besides, it's definitely not your fault if her technicians were incompetent. Well, that's another crime for which you get to judge her today. Today's examination is definitely for Shiatsu's sake. We need to confirm something about you before we can make an informed decision."

Alex: "What do you need to know about me?"

Matriarch: "Do you know what a 'hermaphrodite' is?"

Sega: "It's an animal that has both genders, male and female. Wait… are you saying that Alex is…"

Matriarch: "It's what a certain someone who's been very intimate with Alex is telling me, and that's what we need to confirm. If he is, it would certainly help in the search for a 'donor' or 'surrogate.'"

Alex: "All right. I'll do it, but I would like my girls with me."

Matriarch: "I was just about to suggest that. I want you to be able to trust me, even a little bit. After that, we're going to be recording a tour of the facilities to broadcast later, then some reporters will be coming to interview you, all of you. Shiatsu won't be getting any reporters since she's in the infirmary under a strict 'no visitors' policy that I put in place. Any reporter who tries to violate that will face severe sanctions. The interviews will be followed by lunch, and then you get some R&R before Alex's wish and Former Matriarch Udderweis' punishment is broadcast live. No, don't tell me your wish. I don't want to know. Let me be surprised just like everyone else."

After eating a light breakfast, we go get Alex's exam. He does indeed have a uterus, but no ovaries, which makes his rather ample bosom a complete mystery. Perhaps he once had ovaries, but they atrophied somehow?

Well, at least the important part is there; now we have to prime it.

Matriarch: "OK, Alex. I've got good news and bad news. The good news, you have a womb. We might be able to transfer Shiatsu's children to you." Everyone starts cheering and celebrating. "The bad news is you don't have any ovaries to go with it. This means your body has not been maintaining a fertility cycle."

Matriarch: "We need to start a hormone regiment to get your uterus ready for Shiatsu's children or the transfer will fail. That means daily shots for a week. Shiatsu is still going to be bedridden."

Alex: "Any the side-effects?"

Matriarch: "I'm not going to lie, Alex. The closest precedent to what we're about to do is hormone replacement therapy for transgender individuals. We can't really be certain of what's going to happen. What I can tell you is that the record of side effects includes nausea; hair growth/loss in strange locations; mood swings, sometimes violent; sleep cycle disorders; tenderness in the breasts; and all sorts of strange changes to the genitals. In short, it's probably not going to be a very pleasant experience for you. Do you still want to do this?"

Alex: "If the alternative is having Shiatsu and my children die, then yes, I'll do it."

Matriarch: "All right. Let's get this started."

I administer the first shot. He seems to take it well, at first. There's no rash or allergic reaction, and that's a good sign. Unfortunately, a half hour later, he begins showing the side effects I mentioned: severe nausea, mood swings, and fatigue equivalent to someone whose circadian rhythm has been disrupted. In a couple of hours, the worst passes, though for the rest of the day, especially during the interviews, he just cries randomly for no reason. I am later told that he was always sensitive to his emotions and gets overwhelmed by them very easily. To his credit, he manages to pull himself together for the important "wish" ceremony and the time when he will be judging Matriarch Udderweis.

When all the girls get dressed in their finest, Alex wears the wedding dress he was reported wearing on the day after the choosing. "It's what my brides chose for me, and what 'she' would have wanted.

It would have been nice having her here in her tux. She was really looking forward to it."

Of course, "she" means Shiatsu who can't be in attendance due to her injuries and the treatments. Although she is watching from her bed, and we've prepared a hologram of her, wearing the tux to stand by Alex, it's just not the same.

The entrance has the live audience gasp in awe. Some people murmur about Alex in a dress, but then they get corrected by their neighbors.

"Among his brides are Shinobi of the Street Scorpions and Shiatsu of the Street Vipers. If they tell me, 'Wear a wedding dress with a padded bra,' then I will wear a wedding dress with a padded bra!" NOBODY complains about the hologram of Shiatsu in a tuxedo. She makes the tuxedo look good. I then make the official winner announcement.

Matriarch: "The winner of this year's Harem Games is Alex Dolorean, and with him are now twelve brides: Sega, Sierra, Atari, Diana, Shinobi, and Shiatsu, who due to her injuries can't be here in person, and the survivors from Tendo Akaneda, Okabashi, Laguna, Panama, Virginia, Monica, and Zori! Let's give them a round of applause!" Everyone cheers for him loudly, everyone except Former Matriarch Udderweis.

Former Matriarch Udderweis: "Little sissy boy's been crying himself to sleep at night?! HAHAHA!"

She makes this taunt as she is brought before the crowd, in chains.

It's obvious to everyone that Alex has been crying due to the hormone- induced mood swings, but only Alex, his brides, and I know that. Udderweis's taunt must be an attempt to enrage Alex to the point that he loses control and forfeits his victory. He's not falling for it though, and neither is the audience. They "boo" quite loudly at her remarks.

Alex: "FORMER Matriarch Udderweis is here in chains because she stands accused of desecrating the Holy Harem Games. The Matriarchy, in the wisdom granted them by the Goddess, has appointed the winner, me, as the one to judge and execute her punishment. I will do so once the evidence is presented before you. Madam Matriarch, if you would be so kind. Could you show the citizens of the empire what she has done?"

Matriarch: "Yes. Here is the security footage recorded during Matriarch Udderweis's tenure showing her misdeeds. After a very thorough investigation, I also found these additional recordings in Matriarch Udderweis's possession."

Everything from the night Alex was taken from his mother's arms, and her illegal arrest, to the "examination," to the attempted cover-up of the beating, to the armed invasion of Alex's hospital room, to even the smashing of the control panel before Sega baptized Shiatsu was shown to the world.

At this point, nobody criticizes Alex's wild mood swings. Being made to watch yourself being violated and abused can (and has) broken even the most stalwart of soldiers, soldiers who have been trained to resist torture. Alex has not, and he's still suffering from the effects of his hormone therapy shot.

When the playback is over, and the audience is obviously shocked and awed, Alex angrily walks up to Former Matriarch Udderweis and simply asks two questions.

Alex: "What have you done to my mother?" and "Is there ANYTHING you want to say in your own defense?"

Former Matriarch Udderweis: "HAHAHA! Stupid little brat! If your mother is not dead, she will be soon! It's what she deserves for humiliating me, and what you deserve for killing my son. You should have known your place and worshipped at my feet. That's all you're good for, you freak! I'm so far above you, I might as well be your god!"

Alex: "Virginia, I'm going to need a tree, cross shaped, about thirty or so feet high, with the top branches strong enough to hold this 'woman's' arms. Can you do that?"

Virginia: "Oh, I know what you have in mind. I think I can."While Virginia is preparing the tree that's going to be used, Alex begins laying out the details of his sentence. "There is legal precedence for this situation. In the ancient Roman Empire, a man was brought before Pontius Pilate charged with the crime of calling himself a god. Although Pilate found him innocent, the Roman Empire, and the Pharisees of the time had the accused tested for his divinity. I don't have all the tools or the time needed for the preamble, so we're going to skip straight to the main event."

Virginia: "All done. I didn't have willow or oak, so this cherry tree will have to do."

Alex: "Are the top branches strong enough to hold her?"

Virginia: "Yes. They should be."

Alex: "Good. Fortunately this dress has a low-cut back. I'd hate to have to ruin it." Alex then grows his steel dragon wings, and carries Former Matriarch Udderweis to the top of the tree.

Former Matriarch Udderweis: "What are you doing, worm?! Put me down!"

Alex: "Now I see where he got it. Your son was just as bad at paying attention as you. Had you been listening, you would have realized that since you JUST claimed you are a god and everyone, including the Matriarchy, should bow before you, I'm compelled by ancient law to test your statement."

Alex then transforms the chains on her wrists and ankles into spikes and crucifies Former Matriarch Udderweis LIVE.

Alex: "Unfortunately, I didn't have the time to have you whipped, beaten, put a crown of thorns on your head, or make you drag this cross up a hill. I sincerely apologize for that. I hope it doesn't affect the test too much. Now I'm told that it could take up to three days for you to die, and each breath is an exercise in pure agony. We don't have to broadcast that, although it gives you plenty of time to reflect on the suffering you yourself have caused, or your subordinates have caused in your name. That's not the clincher. The clincher is that he managed to resurrect himself after being buried for three days after dying like this. So, if you can somehow resurrect yourself and open your sealed tomb from the inside, then we'll talk about your divinity."

He flies down and lands back on the stage, Udderweis screaming all forms of obscenity at him all the while.

Alex: "I don't mind. Please keep screaming, yelling, and ranting your self-serving vitriol. It will only increase your agony so much more."

Udderweis falls silent at that, and concentrates on just staying alive, trying to minimize her pain.

Alex: "Madam Matriarch, I hope for your sake what she said is not true. Right now, I have no grudge against you, personally, but I do have an oath to uphold, and as long as you are a member of the Matriarchy, I would have to consider you an enemy for my mother's sake."

Matriarch: "I understand, and we'll go find your mother after you have made your wish."

Alex: "Then my wish is simple, and I know it's within the Matriarchy's power."

Matriarch: "What is it?"

The audience grows silent.

Alex: "In honor of Tendo Akaneda, I hereby wish for the Harem Games to end, PERMANENTLY!"

The audience immediately erupts. Nobody criticizes Alex especially after just seeing what he went through, but nobody is exactly jumping for joy either. The Games have become a centerpiece of the Empire's culture; to suddenly have it taken away is a huge shock. That was masterfully played, Alex. I'm glad I asked you not to tell me beforehand. Now my surprise and shock is genuine. More than that, I am more than a little pleased. I have always hated the Games. For the first time in two hundred years, a winner is actually looking out for those who have come before and those yet to come, not just for himself. As matriarch though, I have to ask these questions.

Matriarch: "What about your brides? You can't keep them like this."

Sega, Atari, Shinobi, Sierra, and Diana immediately reply. "We want to stay with him. We are not going anywhere, and by law we can't be taken away by force."

Matriarch: "And as for you, former brides of Tendo Akaneda?"

"It was our late husband's last wish that we go with Alex. Although we never found our husband 'sexy,' we knew that he was always looking out for us. Besides, we know that Alex knows how to treat his ladies. We are going to stay."

Matriarch: "Can any of you speak for Shiatsu who is not present?"

Okabashi: "I can do better than that. I have a recording of how Shiatsu feels on the matter."

She pulls a recording device out of her blouse. Of course, I know the recording device is meaningless and she's actually using her powers, but I say nothing. Shiatsu's image appears before the audience and the cameras. Everyone falls silent as her love confession plays out for all to hear.

Shiatsu: "Alex, when we first met, I was sent to you as your whore, not your bride. I was sent only for the sake of collecting your seed. Since that failed, I was ordered to take your children, by subterfuge or by force. When you learned of this, it would have not been surprising if you looked upon me with hatred or contempt. Instead, you rushed forward to protect my body, my virtue, what little of it remained, and eventually even my soul without asking for anything in return. You have introduced me to five absolutely wonderful women who have been nothing but generous and kind to me, including Shinobi who should have had good reason to hate me, and when we made love, it was in the most gentle and intimate way possible. There is absolutely no doubt in any fiber of my being that I am your most precious person. Even though my soul belongs to almighty God, my heart, my mind, and my body are all yours, now and forever. I, absolutely, am not going anywhere. Woe be onto anyone who tries to take me."

Everyone in the audience is stunned. Whispers like "a confession of absolute loyalty from Shiatsu of the Street Vipers? He must be one hell of a husband/lover." reverberate through the crowd.

Alex: "I think that answers everyone's feelings on the matter. Would you not agree, Madam Matriarch?"

Matriarch: "What about where you will live? What will you do?"

Martufe: "I can answer that. There was a very old living will assigned to me when the Games first began. It states that should a winner actually wish for the Games to end, the arenas, all of them, and everything in them would be his property, tax and duty free, for the rest of his life. The Matriarchy signed off on this long ago, valid in perpetuity. Alex, everything I own is now yours. All I ask is that I stay on as caretaker until I finally die, decide to leave, or you master running things, whichever comes first."

Alex: "Well, that answers that."

Matriarch: "But there are so many bad memories here."

Alex then puts his arms around his brides. "And quite a few good memories too. Without the 'tournament,' this is a beautiful place to live. I am also not naïve. I know there's going to be quite a bit of resentment aimed at me from the families of those who are no longer here, and I can't think of a more secure place for me or my family."

The audience goes silent at that. Nobody EVER gave thought to the "losers" before or their families. Alex just reminded EVERYONE of the thought that people died for the amusement of some elites on a throne somewhere.

Alex: "The only thing missing is my mother, who was promised to me, alive and well, should I win the Games."

Suddenly Okabashi yells "GUN!"

We all dive as a sniper shot rings out, missing my head by seconds. Okabashi replays the message she heard.

"Kill the traitor, then everyone else there. We will NOT grant the winner's wish under any circumstances."

The "security" for the event turns their guns on us, but Alex is faster. He fries them where they stand with a water-led lightning bolt.

Alex: "Sega, Sierra, Diana, go with the matriarch to the hover car bay. I need the three of you to escort her to my mother; you can expect heavy resistance. Martufe, I need those referee bots to repel the hostiles."

Martufe: "Already done."

Snipers surrounding the stage begin dropping like flies as they are out-sniped by the mechanical wonders who refereed the last round of the Games.

Alex: "Okabashi, Virginia, Laguna, Zori, Panama, Monica. I need you to head to the hover car bay also and plot a trip to Exile Island. If we're going to take this fight to the Matriarchy, we're going to need troops, and that's the best place to get them, if the Matriarchy hasn't attacked there already."

Matriarch: "If you're going there, look into bringing the inmate, Notoria Elderbairns. Her assistance will be invaluable in Shiatsu's care."

Alex: "You heard her, secure Exile Island, and bring as many inmates as you can back here, but the priority will be Notoria Elderbairns. Atari and Shinobi, go to the medical bay and protect Shiatsu. The guards are supposed to be working under Martufe, but they are completely unreliable."

Matriarch: "But the medical bay is in lockdown."

Alex: "Former Madam Matrirarch, they can break the doors down at any time. I speak from experience; the medbay is not secure."

Atari begins shaking with terror. "I can't, Alex. I'm sorry. I just can't. My powers... They... They...!"

Alex holds Atari's face firmly but gently and looks into her eyes. "Yes, you can. I believe in you. I trust you. You are stronger than this. You are stronger than your fears. You are MUCH stronger than those despicable cowards who hurt you. You can overcome ANYTHING you put your mind to. That is why I love you." He then kisses her passionately.

Atari: "I... understand. NOBODY will get to Shiatsu!"

Alex: "Martufe, come with me off stage. I need to change. After that, go to the medbay and help with the defense. Matriarch, please stay with me a moment before you go. I need some information from you."

Martufe: "Change? What do you mean? And where will you be going?"

We all head backstage. Shockingly, Alex begins stripping himself naked.

Alex: "Martufe, please take this outfit to Shiatsu. It has a lot of sentimental value, and I don't want to ruin it. Don't look so shocked, Former Madam Matriarch, it would be idiotic to think there's anyone, including yourself, who hasn't already seen me completely naked."

Matriarch: "Eldorado. My name is Arcadia Eldorado."

Alex: "A true honor to learn your name, Lady Eldorado. Now can you tell me where your family is staying? I know you alone won't be targeted for death today. You were called a 'traitor' just now."

That's RIGHT. The Matriarchy doesn't just execute 'traitors;' they execute the whole family. How does Alex know that?

Alex: "As you may or may not know, I had a little chat with

Contestant Tendo Akaneda, and I gathered that the Elite don't just go after 'traitors' but go after the whole family. Am I right?"

Arcadia Eldorado: "You are correct."

Alex: "Then in that case, can you tell me the way to where your family is staying, 'as the crow flies?' I am going to rescue them, or at least give the Elite hell trying!"

Arcadia: "Why? Why would you do that for me?"

Alex: "Three reasons. 1.) I haven't known you long, but you've been good to us, or at least fair. That deserves a reward. 2.) I know what it's like to be torn from my mother's arms, and I don't want your innocent children to feel the same. 3.) I OWE those 'Elite' some serious payback, and the Matriarchy needs to learn that they are not 'goddesses' to be worshipped. Oh wait, that's four reasons, isn't it?"

Arcadia: "'Thank you' just doesn't seem enough."

Alex: "Just take good care of Shiatsu, my children, and my mother if you can, and we'll call it even."

Arcadia: "Deal." I give him the most direct areal route to my house as well as our family's secret code, and he transforms into his dragon form and flies off there like a flash while I head to the hover car bay with Sega, Sierra, and Diana to try and rescue his mother.

TO BE CONTINUED IN "The Anointed Prophetess."

Credits:

Author: Jorge L. Carreras Jr. @2012

Jorge L. Carreros p.

CPSIA information can be obtained
at www.ICGtesting.com
Printed in the USA
FFOW02n0628071014
7849FF